"Yes or no . . ." Chelsea whispered
  seductively.

"Will you write a song for me, Dakota?"

"I'll think about it," he said coolly.

This was an obvious brush-off. A flash of
fire flickered in Chelsea's eyes.

"You do that," she said. Then, standing
on tiptoe, she proceeded to kiss Dakota
senseless, repaying him in kind with a kiss
that was insultingly thorough, blatantly
sexual and deliberate in message.

It said, *I don't give an inch. And I'm not
giving up on you.*

Just like her heroine Chelsea Stone—
a bad girl you'll fall in love with—author
Tiffany White won't take no for an answer.
This is her seventh Temptation novel—all
inspired by a rejection letter she once received
from another publisher years ago. She
promptly quit her job to write full-time—
with outrageously successful results.

Books by Tiffany White

HARLEQUIN TEMPTATION
367—FORBIDDEN FANTASY
407—DARK AND STORMY KNIGHT
442—BAD ATTITUDE
465—NAUGHTY TALK

LOVE, ME
TIFFANY WHITE

Harlequin Books

TORONTO • NEW YORK • LONDON
AMSTERDAM • PARIS • SYDNEY • HAMBURG
STOCKHOLM • ATHENS • TOKYO • MILAN
MADRID • WARSAW • BUDAPEST • AUCKLAND

For my friend Donna Julian
who inspired this story and
co-conspired No. 6 Gadsby Street

and

Chelsea Meyer...Miss America in training

ISBN 0-373-25590-X

LOVE, ME

Prologue

CHELSEA STONE STOOD outside the Nashville store where everyone who was anyone in the country-music business shopped for boots. She pretended interest in her scarlet nails while Dakota Law, country music's brightest star, took his own sweet time surveying the damage she'd done to his car.

From the corner of her eye, she saw his jaw clench in irritation. His bad mood rather surprised her; only a junkyard owner would consider his clunker of a car a prize.

A more prudent woman would have left a note on his windshield and fled. A more timid woman would now quail at the tightness in Dakota's wide shoulders and the belligerence in his stance.

Timid and *prudent* weren't adjectives anyone would apply to rock music's bad girl, however. Everything from her mane of wild black curls and pouty red lips to her flashy long legs was part of the carefully cultivated image of seductive rebelliousness calculated to help her compete successfully with the rude boys of rock and roll.

Living up to that image of female aggressiveness, Chelsea had gone inside the store to track down the car's owner. In reality, she only rebelled against senseless rules.

At first Dakota had thought she was flirting with him and the story of the crash was a come-on. She'd soon set him straight about that and he'd followed her outside.

Dakota Law was too young to be a legend, but he was one nevertheless. A Southern singer/songwriter of country love ballads, everything he produced rode to the top of the bestseller charts.

He turned on his booted heel to face her.

"Oopsies," she responded to the look of fury in his dark blue eyes. He had enough hair for a ponytail, but probably not enough guts, she thought irreverently.

"You demolish my car and 'oopsies' is all you can say?" he asked, incredulous. He tipped back his white Stetson with his knuckle.

"I . . ." She started to explain, but he turned back to the disreputable reject with fifties fins and a color scheme of turquoise-and-gray primer. He kicked a tire, no doubt wishing it was her. "I can't believe you wrecked my car," he said, turning back to face her.

"How do you wreck a wreck?" she demanded, undaunted by his theatrical show of machismo.

His eyes narrowed. "It may not be much to you, but this car is important to me. It has sentimental value."

"In that case I'll pay you twice what it's worth," she said, whipping out her checkbook. She wrote out a check, signed it with a flourish and offered it to him.

"Fifty dollars? Are you nuts?"

"Probably, but I'm feeling generous," she replied, deliberately misinterpreting him. She'd gone from feeling contrite when she'd demolished his car to feeling irked by his unreasonable attitude—an attitude that no doubt had a lot to do with her.

"I don't want anything from you," he said, his tone clinching her assessment. "All I want to know is how in the hell you managed to wreck the entire side of my car."

"If you must know, I was listening to this song playing on the radio . . ." she began, inventing hastily, not wanting him to know she'd swerved to avoid hitting a dog.

"Oh, that explains everything," he said, slanting her a sarcastic look.

Chelsea went back to studying her nails. "It sure does, cowboy. It was one of your songs I was listening to and it put me to sleep at the wheel."

He let her smart-ass remark ride.

That he could take it as well as dish it out scored a point with her in his favor. She put her checkbook away.

"What is someone like you, someone used to the fast track, doing moseying around in Nashville, anyway?" Dakota asked.

"Buying boots, same as you." She smiled. So he'd recognized her.

"I hope you use them for walking out of here and back to L.A. where you belong. I never want to see you again, lady."

"And here I thought you were smarter than the average cowboy," she taunted, tearing up the check and letting the bits flutter onto the street.

"What are you talking about?" he asked, looking puzzled.

"The check," she explained. "My autograph alone is worth twenty times the value of your stupid car."

"Not in my book, lady. Now will you please just go."

"Later," she said with a cavalier wave as she climbed back into her rental car, unconcerned about its badly crumpled right-front fender.

Adjusting the rearview mirror as she drove away, she saw him kick the tire again, then throw down his cowboy hat in utter disgust.

She'd gotten his attention, no matter how unintentionally.

Now she had to play her bad-girl image for all it was worth, pretending a confidence she didn't have.

DAKOTA FELT LIKE A bastard.

His bad day hadn't been entirely her fault, yet he'd taken all his frustration out on her. It didn't matter that her attitude had rankled him. And if the truth be told, it may even have excited him a little. But he'd been raised to be a gentleman. There was no excuse for rudeness.

The next time he saw Chelsea Stone, he'd apologize.

Maybe even buy her dinner.

But not because he was interested.

Because he wasn't. Chelsea Stone would eat him for breakfast.

And then he smiled. He supposed there were worse fates.

1

CHELSEA STONE STOOD offstage awaiting her turn at the microphone. She hadn't had a hit record in some time, but that didn't matter at the Farm Aid benefit. This was a one-shot performance doing two or three of her biggest hits with her old band.

The fact that she was a rocker didn't make her out of place at the essentially country benefit. Neither did her black Harley-Davidson T-shirt, matching baseball cap and skintight jeans. The Farm Aid benefit was a loose mix of performers of everything from country to hard rock, all pitching in to help save the family farms. She'd seen Willie, Axl and dozens of artists from several music genres.

But she hadn't seen *him*.

"Have you seen him?" she asked Tucker Gable, the lead guitarist from her old band.

The rumor mill had pegged Tucker as her lover. He'd formed his own band a year ago—before her throat surgery to remove a couple of benign growths on her vocal chords—but she and Tucker were still close.

"Seen who?" Tucker asked, fiddling with the small gold hoop in his ear.

"Dakota Law," she answered. John Mellencamp nodded as he brushed past Chelsea on his way to the stage.

"Why are you looking for Dakota Law?" Tucker asked. "Or is it that you're looking out for him? You still trying to avoid running into him because you wrecked his car?

"Relax babe. I don't think the dude will be carrying a grudge over something that happened months ago. Besides, you told me it was an accident. It's not like that time we hid the Mindbenders' instruments when we were on tour."

"I'm not looking to avoid Dakota, I'm looking to find him, Cheesebrain."

Tucker ignored her pet name for him. With his romantic long blond hair and bare chest beneath his trademark black leather vest, he looked like a dim bulb. He wasn't.

"Ah ..." Tucker wrapped the word with meaning as he gave her a considering look. "Should I be worried about you? Have you gone sweet on him?"

"Sweet on—"

"Oh, don't go getting your knickers in a knot, babe. I was only teasing. I know I'm a hard act to follow." He winked broadly. "Nearly impossible, wouldn't you say?" he added insufferably.

"Why don't you go find a mirror to play with?" Chelsea retorted, punching his hard, tattooed biceps good-naturedly. The tattoo was a tiny rose with the name Chelsea done in script beneath it.

Chelsea and Tucker were each other's only support system in one of the most unstable businesses. They had each left an abusive home at an early age, and were alone in the world. Tucker had had his tattoo done to show her he would always be there for her.

Chelsea had balked at a tattoo at first, but had finally given in to the sentiment—sort of. Her tattoo was located on the inside of her ankle and was an even smaller rose with Tucker's name ribboned around it. It was only noticeable up close and legible only upon very close inspection.

The first time Tucker had seen the inscription, he'd laughed out loud.

It read . . . Cheesebrain.

"Quit doing that," Tucker said, rubbing his arm. "It's not good for my image to have women hitting on me—well, not that way, anyway."

Mellencamp finished warming up with his band and launched into "Paper and Fire." The huge crowd swayed with the music as he boogied across the stage, his snake-hipped moves similar to Jagger's and Axl Rose's.

Chelsea and Tucker enjoyed the class-reunion feel of the benefit. They picked up their abandoned conversation after Mellencamp's "Rain on the Scarecrow" finale and his appeal for donations for the heartland of his roots.

"So," Tucker teased, his eyes twinkling, "why exactly are you looking for 'Da Law'?"

"I'm not entirely certain I want to tell you."

Tucker shook his head. "You have to tell me, Chelsea."

"Why?"

"Because we tell each other everything, babe. Remember?"

It was true. They did tell each other everything. They'd picked up the habit of sharing their lives early on when they'd met as runaway teenagers. They had left the nightmare of abuse to follow their dreams and neither had ever looked back. Their success in the music business had been improbable, but their talent, guts and determination had made their luck happen.

"If you must know," Chelsea said with a sigh, "I want to do a little business with Dakota."

"Business?" Tucker's brow furrowed. "What kind of business? He's a country singer, not a rocker.

And from what you said about his attitude, I don't think he's a paid-up member of your fan club."

Chelsea shrugged. "He doesn't have to like me to write a song for me."

"A song? You're kidding."

"No, I'm not kidding. Much as I hate to admit it, everything he writes is a hit. Something I could really use right now. In case you haven't noticed, since the surgery my songs have been moving in the wrong direction on the charts...at ballistic speed."

"But Dakota Law only writes ballads—*country* ballads."

"And maybe I can sing them. With the warning my doctor gave me about doing any more damage to my vocal chords, I don't have much choice about changing what I sing. Even the songs we're doing today I picked because they were the least taxing.

"Besides, country music has changed. Heck, look at Garth Brooks. He hit number one over rap and rock and soul. The lines between country and rock are blurring, anyway."

"You really think your public will accept a softer image of Chelsea Stone?"

"Why not? I'm a woman, aren't I?"

"Oh yeah, you're a woman. But—"

"But what?" she asked, looking at him through narrowed eyes and flicking her dangerous red nails as she waited for his reply.

"I don't scare easy, remember?" Tucker said with a laugh. "Put down your weapons. I was only saying that you built your career on being a bad girl. Do you really think your fans are going to accept you as sweet and innocent like the women who sing Dakota's songs?"

"No, but there must be a middle ground. My throat has healed but I can't go on abusing it like I used to. And I can't not sing. I think Dakota can help me."

"Yes, but will he?"

"Why wouldn't he?" she asked, as The Beach Boys took the stage.

"Because he can pick and choose the women who sing his songs. I hear he's very particular."

"So am I." Behind her bad-girl image lay a perfectionist—something only Tucker knew. It took tremendous drive and willpower to maintain her public image. In public, she was never seen or photographed not looking like "Chelsea Stone," the reigning female pop star of the past decade.

Tucker shook his head. "You aren't going to let him say no, are you, babe?"

"Did I let you?"

"No. No, you didn't," he agreed, hugging her affectionately.

"I know it's not going to be a piece of cake, Tucker. You have any suggestions how I might get Dakota to write a song for me? I'm all ears."

Tucker looked at her closely. "What? You're listening to my advice, all of a sudden?"

"Enjoy it. It won't last."

"No shit, Sherlock."

"Come on, Tucker. You're a guy. What would get you to write a song for me?" she persisted, as the crowd joined The Beach Boys in their most famous surfing song.

He pulled her closer and leaned down to whisper in her ear, then gave a rich and raunchy laugh at her reaction. A blaze of scarlet stained her face.

"Tucker Gable, you should have your mouth washed out with soap."

"Well, you asked," he said, tears of merriment leaking from his eyes.

"Okay, besides *that*, you pervert."

The Beach Boys were on about their fifth go-through of the surfing song. "Looks like they're going to have to get the hook," Tucker said with a nod. "Once you get a sixties group onstage, it's all over."

"I like The Beach Boys," Chelsea said in their defense, not that they needed any from the cheers of appreciation coming from the crowd.

"So do I, but I'd like to get onstage and do our set in this lifetime."

"Forget about The Beach Boys, will you? They don't need your help and I do. What should I do about Dakota?"

"Why don't you just ask nicely. That would be a novel approach for you."

"And if that doesn't work?"

"Then do what you always do," he said, slapping the hand of Brian Wilson as he came offstage.

"What I always do?" Chelsea looked puzzled. "What are you talking about?"

"You know, do what you always do to get your way—pester the hell out of him."

"I never . . ."

"Really?" Tucker's eyebrow rose. "You didn't leave dozens of notes and small tokens of your esteem for me when you were trying to get me to head up your band?"

"But that wasn't pestering."

"It wasn't?"

"No, that was nurturing, building up your self-esteem. I know you don't like to admit it, but you needed that. Everyone does."

"Chelsea, I was saying no and you wouldn't listen."

"That's because I knew how good we'd be together. We are good together, aren't we, Tucker?" She trailed a flirty nail down his biceps.

"The best, babe," he said, lifting her hand to his lips and gently kissing her palm as the stage manager signaled they were next onstage.

DAKOTA LAW STOOD OFF to one side, about twenty feet away, watching Chelsea and Tucker's affectionate love play. Chelsea Stone was hotter than a bubbling cauldron—an apt description since she seemed to have put some sort of spell on him. His life had pretty much gone to hell in a handbasket since their inauspicious meeting six months ago in Nashville.

He'd changed his mind. There weren't worse fates than Chelsea Stone. He planned to steer clear of her.

Her hot rock and roll belted out in a husky alto bravura was not his style at all. She was not the kind of lady he approved of. With a great deal of effort he tried to force his gaze from the exhibitionistic fit of her jeans and the spot where Tucker Gable's hand rested on them.

But he couldn't stop watching Chelsea and Tucker flirt outrageously onstage as they did their songs. They were a matched pair of gorgeous rebels.

And the songs were as sexy as rock and roll got—which was saying a lot. Chelsea stood toe to toe with the boys of rock and roll and gave as good as they gave. Women, oddly enough, loved Chelsea; girls from preteens to women several decades older copied her hairstyle, red lips and sexy clothing. They also copied her attitude.

"Ouch!" Dakota swore at the thorn on a misthrown long-stemmed rose that pricked his skin.

Onstage, Chelsea and Tucker were taking their bows as roses rained around them. Maybe her recent records hadn't done so well on the charts, but it was clear Chelsea Stone singing live was another story. All she needed was the right song and she'd be back on top, he knew.

He rubbed his finger over the thorn prick on his neck, licked it and tasted blood. It crossed his mind then that that was what it would be like with Chelsea Stone—she was the type of woman who drew blood from a man.

A smart man would give a woman like her a wide berth. And that was just what he intended to do.

He'd do his bit for the benefit and then head back to Nashville where their paths weren't likely to cross again. She'd already done enough damage.

Deep in thought, he failed to notice Tucker and Chelsea leave the stage.

The next thing he knew, Chelsea was standing in front of him. Tucker was nowhere to be seen.

"Is that for me?" she asked, reaching out to take the rose he was still holding.

"Uh . . . yeah. It's, uh, it's for you," he mumbled like a tongue-tied schoolboy, his eyes darting around for an escape route.

The stage manager gave him one with the signal that he was on next.

"I've got to go," Dakota said, and bolted for the stage. What on earth was wrong with him? It must be the heat. The crowd. Stage nerves.

Tucker returned with something cold to drink to soothe Chelsea's throat and the two of them watched as the crowd cheered Dakota's arrival on-stage. A few of the rowdier fans yelled out requests for their favorite hits from his albums that had gone Platinum in record time.

"Thanks," Chelsea said to Tucker, taking the cold soda he'd scrounged up for her. Tipping it to her lips she began to drink thirstily.

A look of concern crossed Tucker's face when she started to cough a few seconds later. "Are you okay, Chelsea? How's your throat?"

"I'm okay. I just drank it too fast and choked," she assured him.

"You're sure?" he asked, watching her closely.

"Positive. Now, will you stop being such a worrywart. My throat held up pretty well, I think. Of course, I took it easy up there. I knew how tempting it would be to get caught up in the fans' enthusiasm. Thanks, Tucker, for picking up my slack."

"Hey, we're a team, you and I."

"Team, eh? Then I take it you'll cross over with me if I make the switch to the country-music scene," she teased. She knew there was no way Tucker would leave his beloved rock and blues.

"Nice try," he said, shaking his head negatively. "You can be a little bit country all you want, babe. Me, I'm all rock and roll."

"Hmm . . ." Chelsea murmured, watching Dakota adjust the mike after talking to the band. "Do you think he sleeps in that?"

"In what?"

"The white Stetson," she answered, nodding to his headgear.

"You'd have to ask the groupies," Tucker said, flashing her a wiseass grin as he lifted her black Harley-Davidson cap and put it on her head backward.

"He's got groupies?" Chelsea asked, a pout in her voice as she readjusted the cap on her head.

"Now that you mention it, I'm probably the only singer good-looking enough to have groupies," Tucker replied, waggling his eyebrows in an exaggerated leer.

She hit him.

"Will you quit that, woman?" he said, slapping her hand away.

Chelsea laughed. Her punches were the equivalent of a house cat nipping a cougar. "Sorry, I can't oblige you."

"What do you mean? Have you gone daft?" He dodged her fingers poking at his ribs.

"It's part of my job. In case you have a change of heart and decide to do country with me, your head will have to fit into one of those Stetsons. I'm in charge of cutting your ego down to size."

"Yeah, right, babe. And I suppose ole Dakota up there doesn't have a big head."

"You know, I don't think he does. He's more—I don't know—moody. What do you think Tucker? Are all songwriters like that?"

Tucker shrugged, then rested his arm across her narrow shoulders as they watched the crowd respond to Dakota Law. *Respond* wasn't quite the right word—*go bonkers* was more like it.

Their cheers drowned out the lyrics at first.

Dakota wrote his own lyrics and music, and he sang only the songs he wrote. After the first song, the crowd quieted enough to hear him sing the wrenching lyrics of his new hit.

He didn't wear sequins; the Stetson, boots and jeans were the only thing traditionally country about him. His jackets were more Armani than Opry, and the T-shirts he wore beneath them were pure silk.

As she stood in the circle of Tucker's arm, Chelsea wondered what kind of song Dakota would write for her. And he *would* write one for her—of that she was absolutely sure. And not one of the romantic ballads he wrote for other female singers. Those wouldn't do. They were too innocent, too sweet . . . too submissive.

He needed to spend some time with her to be able to write what she wanted.

"You want me to get lost?" Tucker asked, breaking into her thoughts as Dakota took his bows.

"What?" Chelsea looked at him in puzzlement.

"Remember, you're going to ask him to write a song for you when he comes offstage," he explained, nodding to Dakota, who was leaving the stage.

"Oh..." she said, her confidence ebbing now that the moment was upon her.

Tucker leaned down to brush a kiss on her nose. "Just don't tell him to eat dirt and die the first time he says no, like you did to me, babe." With a wink, he disappeared into the crowd as Dakota approached.

Chelsea took a deep breath. She wasn't nearly as strong as she pretended. Please, God, let him agree to write a song for her. She had to get her career back on track.

If she wasn't "Chelsea Stone," who was she?

2

DAKOTA'S EXIT FROM THE stage was stopped by a fluttery female celebrity, breaking unofficial protocol by asking for his autograph.

Chelsea watched his polite smile as he took the woman's pen and honored her request. So, she grumbled to herself, it appeared the cowboy did have a polite bone in his body—just not when it came to her. The woman engaged Dakota in conversation and Chelsea took the brief respite to work on pumping up her nerve. She was insecure, despite her public image of being a tough customer.

It was something only Tucker knew. She'd adopted the commercial slogan Never Let Them See you Sweat as her own professional motto. If the press didn't know where you were vulnerable, they couldn't hurt you.

Not that they didn't try.

There were probably more rumors and bogus tabloid stories about her than any female performer around. She pretended indifference.

What, she wondered, would a shift from rock to country bring? Would she be able to keep it together, to reinvent herself, or were the seams going to show? What would become of her if she failed?

She took a deep breath to quiet her fears.

Dakota had disentangled himself from the persistent fan. He was heading in her direction, then, spotting her, quickly averted his glance and turned at a forty-five-degree angle to avoid crossing her path.

Not only was he rude, he was a coward, as well.

Could he still be carrying a grudge after all these months? It wasn't as if his old car had been some sort of irreplaceable classic; it had been a wreck even before she'd hit it.

Maybe he simply didn't like her. And that didn't bode well for her plans. Not well at all.

How could he not like her? she wondered, both wounded and angered by the possibility. She was a good person. Hell, she was a wonderful person. Well . . . most of the time, anyway.

He could ask Tucker. But somehow she didn't think Dakota would take Tucker's word on much—he'd never get past the fact that Tucker had a tattoo, and worse, that it had her name on it.

Dakota Law was a snob.

He was also a talented songwriter and she desperately needed a hit, so she'll just have to deal with his condescending attitude.

Letting out the breath she'd unconsciously been holding, she called out his name.

Everyone seemed to hear it but him. Everyone turned to look at her but him. Undaunted, she headed after him.

She called his name again, louder this time. More insistently.

Now people were staring at the two of them.

Dakota turned and began working his way toward her before she called any more attention to them.

"You were really good up there," she said when he reached her side. They were still being stared at by the curious performers and assorted backstage personnel.

He touched his hat in a gentlemanly gesture, though his dark blue eyes held a look that was anything but. "Thank you, Ms. Stone, so were you," he managed through clenched teeth. That said, he made a move to end their meeting.

Chelsea put a hand on his arm and moved closer to speak, just as Willie Nelson and Waylon Jennings took the stage. The crowd's enthusiastic cheers drowned out any possibility of conversation.

When the noisy crowd settled down as the two launched into their duet, it was Dakota who spoke. "The answer is no."

"But you haven't . . . you don't even . . . how do you know . . . I haven't even said what I wanted," Chelsea fumed. She wasn't sure if she was hot from the combination of the summer sun and the huge crowd, or from Dakota's impervious manner.

"I'll tell you what, I'll agree to talk to you on one condition—you agree that after I listen to what you have to say, and then tell you no, you'll go."

"How do you know you'll say no?"

"Easy," he drawled in response to her angry retort. "Only a fool would say yes to a woman like you. And I'm no fool, Ms. Stone."

She held her tongue, but just barely.

"Are we agreed?" he prompted, his tone condescending.

She lost it then, and told him what he could do with his "condition."

"I take it 'Eat dirt and die' is your quaint way of saying you don't wish to continue." A ghost of a smile played on his lips.

Chelsea glared at his broad back as he turned and disappeared into the crowd.

"I CAN'T BELIEVE YOU told him that, after I warned you not to," Tucker said when she relayed the outcome of her confrontation with Dakota to him on their flight back to Los Angeles.

Chelsea bit her bottom lip, knowing he was right, but she wasn't in any mood to be reasonable. "He didn't even wait to hear what I had to say. Clearly I don't meet his high standards of womanhood." She snatched up a bag of sugary peanuts from the tray in front of Tucker. The stewardess serving drinks and peanuts had taken one look at Tucker and passed him a couple of extra bags.

Chelsea paled as the Fasten Seat Belts sign came on.

"Just a little turbulence, babe," Tucker assured her, taking her hand.

"I've got to figure out a way to make Dakota listen to me and realize I'm offering him a sweetheart deal," she said.

"I think I know the problem with the sweetheart deal," Tucker said dryly.

"What?"

"You're the 'sweetheart' involved."

Chelsea hit his arm. "I thought you were on my side, Tucker Gable."

"Will you quit that? I am on your side. I love you, but I also know you."

"What sort of crack is that?" she demanded.

"It means you're a high-maintenance woman, is all."

"That's the most ridiculous thing you've ever said."

"It is not. Is it or is it not true that—"

"Tucker!"

He pulled her close and held her in his arms as the plane rose and fell through a patch of nasty turbulence.

Chelsea hated being a white-knuckle flyer. On the whole she was a pretty brave sort, but not being in control frightened her. It was a holdover from the terror she'd felt as a child at the mercy of abusive parents. She refused to be a victim anymore.

She didn't expect anyone to be good to her. That was why Tucker was so dear. He was silly, sweet and considerate, despite his wild-rocker public image.

He stroked her hair, whispering comforting words to soothe her case of nerves. "It's okay now, babe. You can open your eyes," he said finally when the Fasten Seat Belts sign went off.

He considered her as she moved from the safety of his arms. "I can read you like a book. You're not giving up on Dakota, are you? You're going to pester the hell out of the poor jerk to get your way, aren't you?"

"I'm merely going to educate him in the error of his ways," she sniffed.

"Uh-huh, like you did me."

Chelsea groaned. "I can only hope he's a better student."

"Why? What's wrong with me?" Tucker tried to look wounded but looked comical instead.

"You? You eat enough junk food to make it into the junk-food hall of shame. I don't have a clue how you manage to stay so fit."

"Vitamins. And nervous energy."

Chelsea laughed. "You don't have a nervous bone in your body." It was true. No one was more laid-back than Tucker. He could sleep on a tour bus. He could sleep through a tornado. Or a plane crash, she thought as the plane gave a sudden lurch.

"It's okay, just an air pocket," Tucker reassured her as the plane settled back into its smooth flight. "Besides, if I didn't like doughnuts so much, we'd never have met."

That was true enough. She'd worked in a coffee shop after she'd moved to L.A., and Tucker had always conned her into giving him free doughnuts with his coffee. The free doughnuts had led to

Tucker getting her an audition with the local bar band he was playing with at the time.

The rest was rock-and-roll history.

They'd gone from being a bar band to recording a hit album. Then on to a road tour to support the album—and they'd never looked back.

And now Tucker had launched a successful solo career, while Chelsea's seemed to be stalled. She hadn't had a hit since she'd recovered from the throat surgery.

She was going to miss touring with Tucker.

But fate had sent her down a different path. A path that Dakota Law was blocking instead of giving her the breakthrough she needed.

His legions of female fans saw a sensitivity in him she couldn't find. Every time he sang a love song, they melted.

And his taste in women didn't run to women who dressed the way they wanted instead of the way they were expected to. Chelsea knew her look intimidated men because it not only said "in style," it also said "in charge." And it got her the attention she craved.

She thought about what she knew about Dakota, the singer/songwriter. His influences were Hank Williams and Kris Kristofferson—the plaintive delivery of Williams and the soulful lyrics of

Kristofferson. He was in his own way a honky-tonk rebel, eschewing the traditional twang for a smooth-as-whiskey delivery that was understated, yet commanding.

So why, when it came to her, did he behave like an obnoxious, self-absorbed jerk?

Was he threatened by her in some way?

Maybe their collaboration would be good for him. Maybe she could persuade the silky-voiced Texan to loosen up. Maybe she could pull him over to the cutting edge and together they could blur the boundaries of pop music.

They could be good for each other's careers—not that his needed the help hers did. Still, country music had a host of young contenders and it was going to take more than talent for Dakota to stay on the top of the heap. It was going to take something unique to retain his stature.

Country music in the nineties was changing and the heroes of the new country songs had to change along with it. That was one thing she could do for Dakota—she could help him understand a nineties woman.

3

DAKOTA KICKED THE SOFA in his dressing room. Then he slammed a fist into the wall. Damn Chelsea Stone. It was all her fault.

His anger and frustration had been building for months, ever since the day Chelsea had wrecked his car. Like a black cat crossing his path, she'd brought him nothing but bad luck.

He wasn't just angry and frustrated—he was scared. He could almost hear the flap of buzzards' wings overhead as they circled, waiting to feast on the carcass of his once-brilliant career.

Oh, sure, he was still on top for now. But that wouldn't last much longer. He couldn't go on fooling everyone. The lyrics just weren't coming for his new album.

Not only was he unable to write, he was restless and out of sorts. Since the day he'd looked up from the boots he was trying on to see Chelsea standing before him with her jet-black hair, bold red lips and eyes that challenged the world, nothing had been the same.

It was as if Chelsea Stone had pointed one of her blood-red nails at him and cast an evil spell. Then she'd returned to L.A. and her lead guitarist, no doubt leaving all sorts of wreckage in her wake.

He wondered what sort of vehicle Tucker Gable drove. Probably something foreign and fast. Chelsea looked like the kind of woman who would appreciate the speed and precision of a good sports car. She would probably be surprised to learn that so did he. He'd had his share of expensive cars growing up. But his very proper, wealthy Southern family hadn't approved of his ambition to be a country singer. They thought it a waste of a Rhodes scholar. He'd ignored their wishes and had gone off to Nashville anyway.

Broke, he'd worked at a series of odd jobs and lived in that old clunker. It had been his good-luck charm. He had written all his hit records in the back seat before she'd destroyed the car.

Chelsea Stone. He smiled, imagining what his uptight family would think if he brought her home to meet them.

And then he remembered he couldn't go home again.

He'd already done something much worse than date an artist; he'd become one. In a family tree laden with bankers, that was tantamount to burning your birth certificate. They'd disowned him.

His family had never understood his need to explore and express feelings. They'd repressed theirs for generations.

And now he didn't know what he was feeling.

Chelsea Stone had jinxed him. That was all there was to it.

She'd whipped out her checkbook like it was some damn magic wand that would take care of any problem that confronted her. It was an attitude he was familiar with, one he'd been exposed to early on in a family of bankers for whom money was the only thing that mattered.

He'd loved his car.

And no amount of money could compensate him for the damage she'd done.

Sassy as hell, she hadn't hesitated for a second to declare her opinion of him and his precious car, making it very clear she thought they were both overvalued.

Hell, maybe she was right.

All he knew was that he wanted his old junker back, which was an impossibility. By now, it was a cube of compressed iron in some junkyard. The dark-haired vixen had consigned it there with one careless twist of her steering wheel.

Fell asleep at the wheel—his foot. And while listening to one of his songs, she'd said. At least he could sing. Not like her—she didn't sing; she made noise.

He was fairly sure he knew what she'd wanted to talk to him about at the Farm Aid benefit. Fairly sure it had occurred to her that he could write her a hit. Imagine her wanting him to write a song for her. At least she hadn't insulted him by pulling out her checkbook and offering him a check for fifty dollars again.

Thanks to her, he couldn't write her one even if he were crazy enough to want to.

Oh, he'd tried, but every attempt in the past months had been a dead end. He'd tried making excuses to himself, but deep inside he knew the magic was gone. He couldn't write.

Not a note, not a word.

For the first time since he'd started his career, he had writer's block. And since he sang only the songs he wrote, that meant no career.

There was a knock on the door of his dressing room and he called out that it was open.

His assistant, Melinda Jackson, came in with the cold mineral water he'd requested. Drinking some before every performance had become a ritual.

"How's the house tonight?" he asked, taking a long swallow from the green plastic bottle of water.

"It's a packed house like it is every time you perform," Melinda replied, her voice soft and wispy, unlike Chelsea Stone's.

He set the bottle aside and picked up his long, expensively tailored jacket. It was elegant in its simplicity. Dakota's trademark was a quiet, seductive kind of onstage presence.

Sequins like the custom-made Manuel jackets some country stars preferred would have been overkill.

His tight jeans almost were.

"How much longer?" he asked, buttoning his jacket. He wondered how the inexperienced opening act was faring onstage.

Since they were playing the Opry, he'd advised them to go for broke. You never knew who might be in the crowd at the legendary country-music hall. He could still recall what it was like to be an opening act.

Hell, it might not be long before he was an opening act again.

"I'd say their act will wrap in about fifteen minutes," Melinda answered, picking a piece of invisible lint off the shoulder of his jacket.

He'd hired Melinda Jackson because she was the kind of ladylike woman he was used to. Too late, he'd realized she was as socially ambitious as his mother. Her possessiveness drove him crazy at times, but he kept her on because she was good at her job, even though he was sure the secretarial college she'd attended had been more like a girls' finishing school.

It didn't take a rocket scientist to know Chelsea Stone hadn't gone to finishing school, he reflected. Or if she had, she hadn't graduated. Chelsea was the sort to get expelled for being a bad influence on the other girls.

It was hardly fair of him, he decided, to judge her when he was guilty of breaking rules himself; disregarding his family's social code was the reason he wouldn't inherit the Law banking fortune. Yeah, but while he might break rules, he told himself, he didn't flaunt the fact.

Melinda looked up at him with doelike eyes. "Is there anything else I can do for you?" she asked hopefully.

"No, I guess I'd better get backstage," he said, dismissing her.

She seemed about to say something else when a knock sounded on the dressing-room door. The door opened and Dakota's drummer, Burt, took a step into the room, then stopped, blocking the entrance. "There's a lady out here to see you, Dakota."

"Who is it?" Dakota asked, expecting a fan.

"The lady says her name is Chelsea Stone," Burt replied then winked. "And if you ask me, I believe her. She's got some legs."

"That's no lady," Dakota grumbled, his stomach sinking. Now what?

"What does *she* want?" Melinda asked, not bothering to keep the proprietary tone from her voice.

"Tell her I'm not here," Dakota instructed.

"Tell her yourself," Chelsea said, as she quickly ducked under Burt's arm and forced her way into the dressing room.

"What do you want?" Dakota demanded.

His uncharacteristic rudeness got Melinda's attention, and she turned to study Chelsea more closely.

"It's nice to see you, too," Chelsea said, sweetly sarcastic and bold as hell.

"I'm getting ready to go onstage," Dakota said, losing control. He jammed his white Stetson on his head and glared at her from beneath its brim.

"This won't take long," Chelsea assured him.

"I'm waiting," he said, tapping his boot.

"I want to talk to you in private," she said.

"We've been over this before. We have nothing to say to one another, remember?"

"I'm not leaving until we talk," Chelsea declared, walking past him and sitting down on the love seat beside his dressing table.

She glanced at a very interested Burt lounging at the door, and then pointedly at Melinda, who stood practically at Dakota's side. "In private."

Dakota clenched his teeth, stared at the ceiling for a long minute, then sighed. With a shrug, he nodded for Burt and Melinda to leave them alone.

"You want me to call Security?" Melinda whispered, turning her back to Chelsea.

"He's a big boy. I bet he can take care of himself," Chelsea retorted.

Dakota nodded and Melinda followed Burt out the door, closing it behind her reluctantly.

"You must be crazy, lady," Dakota said, taking off his hat and tossing it on the chair.

She might be crazy, but she sure looked good, he thought. Sitting there on the love seat, she looked as if she didn't have a care in the world.

Her pose was unladylike, of course.

She had on a very short, silky, print dress. Her knees were spread wide apart and the dress pooled between thighs sheathed in black tights. She did indeed have "some legs," as Burt had pointed out.

Her feet were encased in red-and-black cowboy boots. He was certain they were the ones she'd bought the day she'd smashed his car. It would be just like Chelsea Stone to wear them simply to annoy him.

His eyes traveled back up her legs past the red-and-white dress to the pièce de résistance—a black leather motorcycle jacket. It had enough zippers to make James Dean hard.

"You're not very good at taking a hint, are you?" he said.

She got up and stood toe to toe with him. Sticking her hands in the pockets of her jacket, she said, "I'd be willing to pay . . . a lot . . . for you to write a song for me."

He wanted to hurt her for the attraction he felt.

Lowering his lips to hers, he gave her a punishing kiss. It was insultingly thorough, blatantly sexual, and deliberately cruel. "What'd you have in mind?"

He expected her to slap him, and was surprised by the sudden tears that gave her eyes a glassy sheen. Just as quickly, they were banished and her tough facade was back in place.

He felt like a jerk.

"Now that you've established you're a bastard, despite your Southern-gentleman image, let's talk currency—because that's the only way I do business." Her words were clipped, her voice icy.

A knock interrupted the heated silence as they took each other's measure. Burt called through the door, "You're on in three."

"What's your answer—will you write a song for me?" Chelsea persisted.

"I'll think about it."

It was an obvious brush-off. A flash of fire flickered in Chelsea's eyes. "You do that," she said, then, standing on tiptoe, proceeded to kiss him senseless, repaying him in kind with a kiss that was insultingly sensual, boldly provocative and unmistakable in message.

It said, *I don't give an inch.*
And I'm not impressed.

CHELSEA WATCHED FROM backstage as Dakota began his opening song after the thunderous applause from the packed audience died down.

It was a torch song, the lyrics all achy and filled with longing. Dakota looked as uncomfortable as hell.

A satisfied smile played on Chelsea's lips when halfway through his song, Dakota did something he'd never done before.

He forgot his own lyrics.

4

CHELSEA STOOD LOOKING out the window of her suite at the Opryland Hotel. The view of the two-acre conservatory was enchanting. Last week's appearance at the Farm Aid benefit, her first live performance since her throat surgery, had netted her an interview with "E Entertainment" and she was in an upbeat mood.

Thankfully the interviewer had kept the tone of the interview light. When the woman asked her why she was in Nashville, Chelsea had hinted at her plans to take her career in a new direction.

She hoped her fans would follow her, but it wasn't something she could count on. Public interest could be very fickle. But if she could bring her old fans and win some new ones—she knew it was a big if—she could be back on top again.

The phone rang.

It was Tucker.

"The interview with 'E' went great," she informed him. "How did your gig go last night?"

"The sound system wasn't the best, but the crowd didn't seem to notice," he answered. "When's the piece going to run?"

"I'm not sure. The interviewer said it would probably air in about two weeks. So, where are you headed next?"

"Somewhere in Iowa, I think."

"Good," she told him. "You'll have time to write letters. Do you have the address here?"

"I always know where you are, babe. How about Dakota? Does the poor bastard know you're in Nashville?"

"He knows."

"And?"

"And he said he'd think about it, just to get rid of me."

"But you're going to try again, right?"

"What do you think?"

"Well, good luck, babe. I've got to run. The band's waiting to go out to breakfast."

"It's two in the afternoon."

"You've been off the road too long—that *is* breakfast time."

"Oh, right, I forgot."

She hung up on his "See you, babe," and stood by the phone for a moment, remembering the camaraderie that was part of being on the road. But she had no time to be blue, she reminded herself. There were suitcases to be unpacked.

And a mind to be changed.

Dakota Law *would* write her a signature song.

When she began unpacking her last suitcase, she came across her mail. She'd scooped it up in her hurry to catch her flight to Nashville. She sorted through it quickly and set aside a small package and a greeting-card envelope.

She opened the small package first and laughed at the ceramic oddities inside. Tucker had picked up the habit of sending her dumb salt-and-pepper shakers from wherever his band played. Putting the package aside, she opened the card. It had a teddy bear on the front.

She smiled. She loved teddy bears. When she'd run away from home her old brown bear had been the only thing she'd taken with her.

She opened the card and read it.

Roses are red,
Violets are blue.
Don't let Dakota
Get to you.

Love, me

THE FOLLOWING EVENING Chelsea made the next move in her campaign to convince Dakota to write a song for her.

He was performing at his club, Dakota Country on Music Row. Chelsea arrived just before he began his last set and prayed that he wouldn't spot her in the audience. She was determined to see him after the performance, sure that if she could get him alone long enough to plead her case, he'd be convinced that writing a song for her was *his* idea.

Chelsea sat at a table as far away from the stage as possible and lowered her head as Dakota strode onstage. When the lights dimmed and Dakota began to sing, Chelsea forgot about being as inconspicuous as possible. She listened breathlessly, and ached and cheered along with the rest of the audience. When the set ended, it took her a moment to remember her reason for being there.

She paid her tab and made her way toward the hallway that led to Dakota's private domain. When she'd entered the club she'd been surprised that the walls were not covered with ego-enhancing mementos of Dakota's stunning career. There was only one picture of Dakota in the foyer; the rest of the wall space was given over to posters of other performers. Autographed posters of Dwight Yoakam, Tanya Tucker and Billy Ray Cyrus were hung outside Dakota's dressing room.

Chelsea hesitated outside the door and listened.

"Can I help you?"

Chelsea froze, then took a deep breath and turned.

"It's you again!" Dakota accused, recognizing her.

"I wanted to talk to you . . ." she began.

"Look," he said, his gaze traveling over her, "I don't care how short that red spandex mini is, the answer is still no."

"But—"

"Stay away from me," he warned, pulling his white Stetson down over his cold blue eyes as he went into his dressing room. The door slammed behind him.

So much for his telling her he'd think about it, Chelsea realized, but she remained standing in the hallway. Her plan of attack hadn't allowed for a door being slammed in her face, but she had no intention of leaving.

She was raising her hand to knock on the door when she heard Dakota begin strumming his guitar. She listened as the strumming went on in fits and starts. With each new start, Chelsea could sense that Dakota was becoming more and more frustrated.

Suddenly he cursed and played a loud, dissonant chord. This was followed by the sound of his guitar hitting the wall. Breaking strings twanged, and then there was silence.

Playing a hunch, Chelsea entered the dressing room without knocking.

"Tell me the truth, cowboy," she challenged. "Is the reason you keep refusing to write a song for me because you *won't* or you *can't?*"

Dakota's head was buried in his hands. "Go away."

"Answer the question and maybe I will."

There was a long pause. "Okay, I can't. Are you satisfied?" he mumbled.

"Why can't you?"

"I thought you were leaving," he said, looking up at her.

"I said, maybe I would."

"Do you try to annoy people, or is it just a natural talent?"

"What I'm trying to do is get you to write a song for me," she said, ignoring his rudeness.

"Well, now you know I can't, why don't you be a good little girl and run along," Dakota replied, nodding toward the door.

"A good little girl? You must be kidding." She took a seat, crossed her legs, and dangled her red high heel flirtatiously.

"Let me guess," she ventured. "You haven't announced a tour date because your album is going to be late . . . am I right? And I annoy you because it reminds you of your problem."

"You are my problem."

"What?"

Dakota unfolded his lanky frame and picked up the ruined guitar. "You heard me. *You* are my problem." He tossed the guitar in the trash.

"What are you talking about? Just because I asked you to write me a song? You've got bigger problems than not being able to write me a song. If you can't produce an album, your record company will toss you out on your rear."

"You're the reason I can't write," he said, snagging her dangling shoe and handing it to her.

"Me?"

"Yes, you."

"I got to you, huh?" Her smile was saucy, her wink sexy.

"No, you got to my car."

She threw her shoe at him. "Will you quit about your stupid car. It was an accident. It was unfortunate, but frankly, don't you think you're just a little bit obsessed about that clunker. It's toast. Get over it."

"I wrote all my hit songs in the back seat of that car," Dakota said flatly.

"You're joking, right?"

"I wish I were," he answered with a resigned sigh.

"Aw, come on. This is an act. You're trying to make me feel guilty, that's all," Chelsea said. What a ridiculous idea that his ability to write hit songs was somehow tied up with an old heap she'd wrecked months ago.

Dakota looked directly at her. "I haven't written a hit song in months. I haven't written a song in months. Not even a chorus . . . a refrain. Nothing, since you smashed my car."

He was serious. She'd wrecked more than his car; she'd wrecked his life—and gone skipping off as if nothing had happened. But how could she have known?

"I'm sorry."

"Are you?"

"Of course, I am."

"You're sorry because I can't write a song for you, is that it?" He picked up her shoe, then knelt down to slip it on her foot.

The words *Prince Charming* came to mind, but she dismissed them. Her career might need rescuing, but she didn't.

"If you were really sorry," Dakota said, when he saw that she wasn't going to be baited, "you'd help me get past my block."

"How can I do that?"

"I don't know. All I know is that since I laid eyes on you . . ." He threw up his hands in a gesture of utter frustration.

"You know you're being superstitious about your car. You *can* write. It's only your mind playing tricks on you. Maybe you should try hypnotic suggestion or something."

"Nope. You caused it, you'll end it. I just have to figure out how."

"Okay."

"Okay? You're agreeing, just like that?"

"Sure, why not? I need you to write a hit for me. If you can't write, I'm out of luck. It's in my best interests to help you get over your writer's block."

Dakota actually laughed.

"What's so funny?" she demanded.

Dakota shrugged. "It's just that I would never have figured you for a pragmatic woman." He looked pointedly at her three-inch red heels. "You certainly don't look like one."

His disapproval stung. "What exactly is your problem? You've been on my case since you first laid eyes on me."

"That's easy," Dakota answered, getting to his feet. "I don't approve of you."

"Well, since I'm not looking for a daddy, it doesn't much matter whether you approve of me or not, does it?"

"You know it wouldn't hurt you to act more like a lady."

She hid the fact that her feelings were hurt. "It wouldn't do a thing for my image. My fans expect me to be outrageous."

Dakota looked at her without comment, then surprised her by asking, "Where are you staying?"

"I'm staying at the Opryland Hotel. Why?"

"So I know where to send someone for your things—if I'm not unblocked by morning."

"Excuse me, I don't recall saying I'd sleep with you, even if you are Dakota Law."

"And I don't recall asking—even if you are Chelsea Stone," he said darkly.

"Then what exactly are you suggesting?"

"I have a ten-acre place that will afford us a lot of privacy about a half hour from here. I'm suggesting that if we spend enough time in close quarters together, maybe you'll annoy me so much, I'll get unblocked just to rid myself of you."

"I don't know how I can refuse such a charming offer," Chelsea said, shooting him a sardonic look. "And for my part, I promise to do my very best to annoy the hell out of you."

"I doubt you'll have to *try*." Dakota mumbled.

CHELSEA RAN HER HAND appreciatively over the soft buttery leather interior of Dakota's new sports car.

"Actually I think you ought to thank me for wrecking your car. This one is a huge improvement," she said.

Her comment only drew a scowl from Dakota.

She tried conversation again. "Do any of your family live with you?"

"No."

Interesting. His no had been both final and unbreachable. She'd have to think about that—later. At the moment, she needed a subject that would interest him.

Since his songwriting was the reason the two of them were hurtling through the star-bright Tennessee night together, it was probably a safe bet. "You really shouldn't worry about it, you know."

"About what?" he asked, glancing over at her.

"Your writer's block. I'm certain the more you keep thinking about it, the harder it will be to break through it. I know it's difficult to be creative when you're anxious about ever writing again. And when you can't come up with any ideas, it's easy to get down on yourself and give up."

"You can put your mind at ease. I'm not giving up. I don't plan on having you for a permanent houseguest. You'll get your song somehow. What I can't figure is why you're fixated on my being the one to write a song for you. Not when your songs are playing on MTV and MTV refers to country music as yee-haw music."

"I'm not thrilled about being forced to make this career change, but as you said, I'm a pragmatic woman. After my throat surgery, I knew I couldn't go on abusing my vocal chords as I had in the past. I knew your romantic ballads would be kind to my throat. Besides, I think it might be interesting to rock some country."

He slid her another glance. "You really think country music is ready for Chelsea Stone?"

"It will be if I'm singing one of your songs," she said, laying on the sugar.

Dakota snorted in derision. "More likely it'll kill two careers with one song."

"I like you, too." Chelsea turned her head to stare out at the black-and-white ribbon of highway unfurled before them. They rode for a few minutes in silence. She considered the reasons why Dakota might be blocked. Was it because he was being too hard on himself? Too impatient? Or was it because he was afraid to fail, afraid of losing the success he'd grown accustomed to? She could certainly relate to that particular fear.

The silence between them began to make her nervous and she reached to turn on the radio.

"I'd rather you didn't," Dakota interjected covering her hand with his. "Hearing other people's music depresses me at the moment."

"Okay," she acquiesced, pulling her hand back to rest in her lap. "I know, let's play."

"Forget it." Keeping his eyes on the road, Dakota added, "I'm not counting out-of-state license plates or anything remotely like that."

"Good grief, what kind of women do you date—and what age? I meant let's play around with some song ideas. You never know, you might come up with a lyric or a good hook for a new song."

"All right," he agreed, but without much enthusiasm. "Go ahead and throw something out."

"Black lingerie, red lipstick and motor oil," she suggested.

"You have a really weird mind. Motor oil . . . where did that come from?"

"We passed a gas station back there. Anyway, the trick isn't to judge the ideas—just to play around with words. Go ahead, you try."

"Go away...don't come back...leave me alone," Dakota declared, glancing over to gauge Chelsea's reaction.

She clapped her hands together in mock delight. "Oh, the hermit song!" Then she shook her head. "Nope, it won't work."

"Why not?"

"Because nothing rhymes with hermit, except maybe Kermit."

"Ah, but you're wrong."

"Name something."

"Okay, how about permit?"

"Use it in a sentence," she challenged.

"Okay." He thought for a moment. "I've got it. You shouldn't be allowed out in that red miniskirt without a permit."

Chelsea bristled. "I've just thought of another word that rhymes."

"What?"

"Cram it."

"Chelsea! I guess there's no hope at all of making you into a lady."

"None."

"It's a shame...."

"Why?"

"Because only ladies sing my songs."

"Maybe that's why you're blocked."

Dakota made no comment on her saucy remark. He stared straight ahead, his lips drawn together in a tight, angry line. The car began to slow and Chelsea wondered a bit anxiously if he was going to leave her on the road, miles outside of Nashville. She relaxed when Dakota geared down and turned into a long, winding drive.

The drive, edged with flower beds, led up a slight incline to a large, pillared house of light-colored brick that sprawled at the top of the hill. A steeper hill was visible behind the house, which, despite its size, nestled gracefully amid trees and gardens. The whole area, including the flower-lined drive, was illuminated with a soft white light.

Chelsea stared around her for a moment, then gave a long, low unladylike whistle of pleasure.

The house was that beautiful—a perfect home for him to bring a debutante to. But a debutante would probably swoon, not whistle, Chelsea thought wryly.

HOURS LATER, DAKOTA sat alone in his kitchen regretting the decision to ask Chelsea Stone to move into his house. What had he been thinking? He hadn't been thinking, that was the problem. He'd been angry about his writer's block and he wanted someone to take it out on. She'd made it easy by accepting the blame.

He tipped his head back and took a long drink of chocolate milk straight from the carton. When he caught his reflection in the chrome toaster on the counter, he smiled. He looked like a kid with chocolate all around his mouth. He felt like a kid, too— like a boy who'd just discovered the attraction of the opposite sex. He'd been all keyed up and unable to sleep since he'd shown Chelsea to her bedroom hours ago.

It had been that line about black lingerie and red lipstick she'd come up with that was to blame. He kept picturing her in nothing but.

Chelsea Stone. If he was entertaining any romantic notions about her, he must be crazy.

There wasn't one area of his life Chelsea would fit into. In her black leather and Chrome Heart accessories, she'd stand out everywhere she went in Nashville.

He imagined what it would be like to take Chelsea Stone home with him. He could just see her wearing her red minidress to one of his parents' charity galas. Hell, if he weren't already disinherited, she'd take care of it in a heartbeat.

Maybe that was why he found her so exciting, he thought, putting the half-empty carton of chocolate milk back in the refrigerator. Chelsea Stone was a woman outside his experience. She could care less that he didn't approve of her, that his family wouldn't. She didn't even seem to realize that she'd have to make some effort to fit into Nashville. It might be the seat of the country-music business, but its atmosphere was that of a small town.

Surely she didn't believe she could flaunt every convention and then win everyone over with his song.

What was he worrying about? There wouldn't be any song. He couldn't write. All his success had been pure luck. He was a fraud just waiting to be discovered.

All he needed was three verses and a chorus. Yet he couldn't string a sentence together, much less a verse.

Let's face it, he didn't really believe Chelsea could actually help unblock him; he'd invited her so he could torture her—pay her back for having wrecked his lucky car.

As he lay in bed an hour later, the provocative image of Chelsea in black lingerie still teasing his mind, he wasn't sure who was the one being tortured.

"Go away...don't come back...leave me alone," he muttered to the image, then punched his pillow and balled it under his head.

CHELSEA COULDN'T BELIEVE Dakota Law had actually asked her to move into his house.

It had been so easy. She hadn't had to scheme or plan; he'd just handed her what she wanted. It disconcerted her.

She stood at the window of the spacious bedroom Dakota had shown her to. It overlooked a small stand of white birch off to one side of the entrance. The delicate leaves on the trees trembled in the gentle breeze. They reminded her of how Dakota made her feel when he turned his clear blue eyes on her.

Maybe it wasn't such a good idea being so close to him. Sometimes when he looked at her as if she were a fancy truffle he shouldn't eat but wanted to, she liked it. But what was his problem? Was he afraid he might like her?

That was it. Dakota was really afraid of her. She smiled. She knew it instinctively.

And she knew why.

She knew from what she'd read about him that his family was in banking, was probably a stereotypical banking family whose men locked up their emotions in the bank vaults along with the money.

But if that was true, then how could a man who came from a cold, unaffectionate family write love songs?

Just maybe, he'd come to realize he was faking it; realize he needed a passionate woman in his life.

Her.

What in the world was she thinking? From the fact that his family was in banking, she'd invented a whole history, a catalog of needs. But Dakota Law was probably better adjusted than she was. Which wouldn't be that hard, according to Tucker.

He didn't need a woman. He had that debutante-type assistant. And fans—thousands of adoring female fans.

Dakota was blocked because he actually believed that stupid car was magic.

He was nuts.

And her career depended on him.

5

CHELSEA HEARD A muffled, distant pounding.

She fought her way up from a deep sleep, but then the sound stopped.

She was drifting gratefully back to sleep when she heard it again.

She opened her eyes and blinked at the unfamiliar surroundings. The noise, she realized, was someone knocking at her bedroom door. This time it was accompanied by a sharp, insistent bark.

"Tucker, is that you?" she called out when the pounding ceased.

"Hell, no," a voice growled on the other side of the door.

Chelsea recognized the voice and the excited yip that had come through the closed door. The annoyed response came from Dakota Law and the playful bark from his black Lab, Pokey.

She wasn't on the road touring with Tucker, and she wasn't in another strange hotel room. She was a guest in Dakota's home. Probably not a very welcome guest, but a guest nonetheless.

"Is this a fire drill?" she called out. It felt as if she'd just fallen asleep.

"Can we come in?" Dakota asked through the door, while Pokey scratched at it and barked.

Chelsea pushed herself up in bed, reached for the quilt and tucked it around her naked body. "Come on in."

The door opened and Pokey bounded onto the bed and licked her face happily.

Dakota, who had just set down Chelsea's bags in a corner of the room, turned to remonstrate the dog.

"Pokey, beha—" he began, then stopped, looking stunned.

Chelsea followed Dakota's gaze and saw that Pokey's playful welcome had caused the quilt to slip, displaying her right breast. "Oopsies," she said, adjusting the quilt.

Pokey plopped down beside her, panting and grinning like she'd known exactly what she was doing, and that maybe there would be a dog biscuit in it for her. Observing the sexy glint in Dakota's blue eyes, Chelsea wouldn't be at all surprised if that was true.

"Uh—" he swallowed dryly "—I had your bags packed and brought them over from the hotel." He nodded toward them. "Breakfast is in half an hour—no room service, sorry. So haul your lazy bones out of bed. Come on, Pokey, let's go."

When man and dog were gone, Chelsea let the soft quilt slip to her waist. The nipples of her breasts had hardened and had a warm, rosy blush to them. She hadn't been as impervious to the desire in Dakota's baby blues as she'd pretended.

She smiled as she shoved back the quilt and got out of bed, not quite sure who was going to drive who crazy during their attempt to get a song written for her.

She made short work of the unpacking, then showered and a half-hour later, descended the stairs for breakfast wearing a white T-shirt with rolled sleeves, a pair of men's boxers worn as shorts, and round sunglasses that were tinted bright blue.

She followed the sound of voices to the airy dining room where she found two things that surprised her. The focal point of the room, a battered oak dining table, was surrounded by mismatched chairs, each wooden curiosity painted a different color.

Even more intriguing, was the fact that seated to Dakota's left, barely visible behind the tall vase of snapdragons in the center of the table, was Melinda Jackson, Dakota's possessive assistant.

Pokey lay near Dakota's feet, her tail thumping on the hardwood floor. Unlike Melinda, the dog was happy to see her. Melinda had shown no surprise when Chelsea entered the dining room, but the look on her face left no doubt that she wasn't one bit happy about Chelsea's presence in Dakota's home.

"Well, you finally decided to join us for breakfast," Dakota said as he stirred sugar into his coffee. "Melinda fetched your things from the Opryland Hotel for me, and I invited her to join us for breakfast. Help yourself to the spread on the sideboard. My cook still thinks he's cooking for my band on tour, so there's plenty."

"Dakota, you should have told Chelsea we dress for breakfast in the South," Melinda chided.

"I am dressed." Chelsea picked up the plate from the place that had been set on Dakota's right.

"Don't you worry what people will think about your dressing that...that way? I would never have the nerve." Melinda's venom was obvious despite the sugarcoating.

"It never occurs to me to worry what people will think of me," Chelsea replied. "I'm more concerned with what I think of them."

Chelsea helped herself to the food on the sideboard. She split a flaky buttermilk biscuit, ladled it with sausage gravy seasoned with pepper, then poured herself a tall glass of tart, pulpy lemonade.

When Chelsea took her place at the table, Melinda began discussing business with Dakota, deliberately excluding Chelsea.

"I've had another call from a firm wanting to sponsor your next tour. What do you want me to tell them?"

Dakota took a sip of his coffee. "What company? You know I've decided against cigarettes and liquor."

"I know. But this is different. The company makes boots, and they want to design a special boot for you to wear while you're performing. You'd get a percentage of every boot sold and they'd pick up the tab for sponsoring the tour, as well."

"Tell them I'll do it, if he won't," Chelsea chimed in, not letting Melinda cut her out of the conversation. She'd decided Melinda would be even more fun to annoy than Dakota.

"I don't think—" Melinda began.

Dakota cut her off. "Chelsea's right, it is an attractive offer. See if you can stall them for a while. I don't want to go out on tour until I have a new album to promote, and as we all know, I still need to write one more song for the album."

Melinda frowned, but made a note on the small pad beside her plate. She toyed with a melon ball, while consulting the rest of her list.

"If you're still having a problem coming up with a new song for the album, I don't see why you don't just cover someone else's song and finish the album. Then you'd be off the hook with your record company," Melinda suggested.

"She's right. And if you don't want to do a new song, you could do a golden oldie," Chelsea added. "Or, I know, why not record one of your old songs with a new arrangement. Something like Neil Sedaka did with 'Calendar Girl'?"

Dakota pushed his plate away and shook his head. "No, it has to be a brand-new song. It's what my fans have come to expect and I'm not going to start disappointing them at this stage of my career."

"But you're already in trouble with your record company because you've missed two deadlines on this album. They're going to suspect you have a serious problem, like drugs or alcohol. They aren't going to be patient much longer." Melinda slipped her list into her briefcase with a look of disapproval on her face.

"Just stall everyone, okay? I'll come up with a new song." Dakota picked up the newspaper and scanned the morning headlines.

"You want to talk about trouble, now those poor people in the Midwest have real trouble," he said as he read the front-page story. "Floodwaters have peeled away entire sections of highway, washed out bridges and knocked out water and power stations. The town of Des Moines, Iowa, is pretty much shut down, according to this."

"Iowa? That's where Tucker is," Chelsea said, tugging the newspaper from Dakota's hands.

"Honestly, neither of you have any manners to speak of," Melinda said in disgust. "You don't read the newspaper at the breakfast table."

"You do if someone you love is stranded in the middle of a natural disaster," Chelsea retorted. She quickly scanned the newspaper's account of the flooding, then passed the paper back to Dakota and excused herself. "I'm going to call Tucker and make sure he's all right."

"Do you think it's wise to have that woman in your home?" Melinda asked, when Chelsea had left the dining room.

"What do you mean?"

"What will people think? Look how she carries on with that guitarist of hers onstage. I've heard their show is shocking when they do concerts together."

"It's only an act," Dakota said, sounding unconvinced himself. "Fans of rock and roll expect to see a sexier show than country-music fans. You can't just stand in one place and sing when you're a rock star."

"That's why rock and roll isn't our kind of music," Melinda sniffed.

"Things change, Melinda. Look at Garth Brooks and his high-energy show. And now that Chelsea Stone is planning to move over to country, I suspect things will really heat up."

"Maybe Chelsea will flop," Melinda said on a hopeful note.

"I certainly hope not. She's going to sing one of my songs."

"You're really going to do it, then? You're going to write a song for her?"

"I'm going to give it a shot. But right now I feel like a game of tennis."

"But I'm not dressed for . . ." Melinda said, looking down at her pastel business suit.

"Oh, no, I meant with Chelsea. I need you to stall off the record company and the boot company. Let me know how you do. I'm counting on you."

"I'll take care of everything. Don't worry," Melinda replied, determined to make herself indispensable to him. Let Chelsea play tennis with him. She would be gone from Dakota's life in a few days or weeks, while Melinda planned to become a permanent fixture.

Excusing himself, Dakota got up from the breakfast table to go and find Chelsea. Melinda remained in her chair for a few moments, dreamily doodling a familiar signature in her mind—Mrs. Melinda Law.

She, not Chelsea, was the right kind of woman for Dakota. It was only a matter of time until Dakota realized the perfect bride for him was right under his nose. She hoped it would be soon. As it was, she'd already changed her mind three times in the past two years about what kind of wedding veil she wanted.

One thing was for certain, she thought, looking around the dining room. These stupid Crayola-colored chairs were going to be the first thing to go when she took over as mistress of the house.

She'd replace them with something tasteful and dignified. Something unlike Chelsea Stone.

Mrs. Melinda Law . . . Yes, that had an impressive ring. A ring that would finally silence her mother's bragging about Melinda's two well-married *younger* sisters.

BACK IN HER ROOM, Chelsea flopped down on the brass bed to place her call to Tucker. She was relieved to hear his voice.

"Tucker, I was worried when Dakota read me the newspaper this morning, and I heard how bad things are in Iowa. Are you and the band okay?"

"Wait—wait a minute, back up. Dakota read you the newspaper this morning? Is that what you said? What's he doing reading you the morning newspaper, Chelsea?"

"Nothing. I've just moved into his house so we can work things out, that's all."

"Work things out? What things?"

"I found out the reason Dakota has been so awful to me is because he's frustrated," Chelsea explained.

"I know the feeling."

"Knock it off, Cheesebrain. He's frustrated because he has writer's block." It had been a relief to know he hadn't disliked her on general principle. That would have been nearly impossible to remedy. But writer's block; how hard could that be to break?

"Writer's block? But what's that got to do with you? I don't understand."

"He's angry with me because I'm the one who wrecked his car."

"That's hardly news, babe."

"I know that. But what I didn't know was that he'd written all his hit songs in the back seat of the car I totaled. And now he can't write anything because he thinks the car was his magic charm."

"So show him some of your magic charm—you know, the stuff you use on me to get your way all the time."

"I do not."

"Right. But what's all this have to do with you staying at Dakota's place?"

Chelsea rolled over on the bed. "I'm staying here because I'm trying to help him get over his writer's block. I feel guilty, Tucker. I'm the cause of it. He blames me." She did feel guilty—not just about the car, but about the fact that most of her concern for Dakota had to do with his inability to help her if he couldn't write.

"And you're really buying this? I think I'd better stop by Nashville and see you after we finish our stop in St. Louis. Ahh . . . oow-weee!"

"What's wrong?"

"Nothing. I'm just sore, is all."

Chelsea laughed. "You'd better retire after your St. Louis gig, Tucker. If playing in a band makes you sore, you're really old."

"I'm sore from sandbagging. The band and I pitched in for a couple of hours to help out. It was the least we could do for a town that gave us a sold-out show."

"Is the flooding really bad where you are?"

"It's pretty awful here in Des Moines. No water to drink, and the power's out, too. You wouldn't believe the damage a flood is capable of doing. The rising water is awesome."

Chelsea heard a knock on the door and a familiar bark. "Hang on a minute, Tucker," she said, then called out to Dakota to come in. Pokey bounded in with typical exuberance, while Dakota remained standing in the doorway. "What's the phone number and address here?" she asked him, then relayed the information to Tucker.

"You be careful driving, Tucker," she admonished. "And be sure to call me when you get to the Riverport Theater in St. Louis, okay?"

"You worry too much, babe," Tucker complained.

"Just promise you'll call me."

"Okay, okay. I'll call as soon as we get into St. Louis tomorrow."

"Good."

"But babe, you've got to promise me one thing, too."

"What?" she demanded.

"That you'll give me a massage when I get to Nashville," he said, groaning.

"Just get here in one piece and I'll give you all the massages you want," she promised, and hung up.

"Tucker's coming here?" Dakota asked, crossing his arms in front of him.

"He's stopping by to see me. You don't mind, do you?"

"No, why should I mind? Tell him to bring the whole band with him. My cook will be thrilled," Dakota said, sardonically.

"It'll just be Tucker. St. Louis is the last stop on this tour, and then they're taking a break."

Dakota didn't seem all that reassured.

"You want to see me about something?" she asked, tossing her hair back.

"I thought you might like to play a game of tennis with me. You do play, don't you?"

"Sure," she lied. How hard could it be to hit a tennis ball back and forth?

"Come on, then, let's go."

She followed him downstairs, through the foyer where a magnificent crystal chandelier hung from the molded ceiling, and outside to the tennis courts located to one side of the balustraded terrace. Pokey accompanied them, running back and forth excitedly.

"Pokey thinks she's the ball girl. She is good at retrieving, I have to admit," Dakota said. He lobbed a ball and told the black Lab to fetch.

Pokey bounded after it, retrieved it and dropped it at Dakota's feet.

Dakota picked up the ball. "The only problem is she slobbers on the balls," he said, wiping his hand.

"I'm sure it won't affect the spin I put on my ball," Chelsea assured him. She wasn't lying, as she hadn't a clue how to put a spin on a tennis ball in the first place. "Let's play."

"Why don't you serve first...."

"You mean because I'm the woman?" she demanded, her eyes narrowed.

"No, because you're the guest, and I'm the gentleman." Dakota tossed two tennis balls her way and she dodged them. Realizing she should have caught them to serve, she bade Pokey go fetch.

Thankfully, the dog returned the balls to Dakota. "Since you have the balls, why don't you go ahead and serve," Chelsea suggested, hoping to pick up a few pointers before she tried it.

Dakota sailed one to her right.

"Wait, I wasn't ready."

She wasn't ready for the entire set. Her serves were mostly double faults. Dakota ran her all over the court, and took enormous pleasure in doing so.

By the time he'd thoroughly trounced her, Pokey was sprawled on the sidelines, her tongue lolling. The only thing that kept Chelsea from joining the dog was her pride.

After Dakota declared game point, Chelsea announced unnecessarily that she guessed her game was a little rusty.

Dakota laughed. "It's so rusty you should get a tetanus shot."

She threw her racket at him.

"Whoa, woman," he said, catching it with one hand. "Anyone ever tell you that you're a bad sport?"

"Not and lived," she grumbled.

"So are you ready for another game?" he asked, pushing his luck.

"Any game but this one." Forgetting her pride, Chelsea collapsed beside the panting dog. When they'd started to play, Dakota had looked like he'd been born to wear tennis whites. He still looked that way, annoyingly so. Why wasn't he sweaty and disheveled?

"You know what your problem is, don't you?" he asked.

"You?"

"No. Well, maybe in a way. Instead of looking at me, you should have been watching the way the ball bounces. It changes direction when it bounces a lot."

"I don't think it matters when you slam-dunk the ball. Haven't you ever heard of a friendly game of tennis?"

"Guess I don't think of you as being particularly friendly," he said, shrugging.

How, she wondered again, could he look so good. He was just moist enough to look inviting, while she, on the other hand, was sopping wet and looking anything but inviting.

She would get even with him.

"What are you smiling about?" Dakota asked suspiciously.

"I'm not smiling."

"Good, because you make me nervous when you smile."

Dakota lowered himself to the ground beside her with a groan.

"Oh, please, I can do without the groaning," she said, hitting him. "You barely worked up a sweat out there on the court."

"Does that mean you're not going to offer me one of your massages?"

Chelsea ignored his question and changed the subject. "Let's talk about the song I want you to write for me."

"Okay," he agreed, his voice lazy and resigned. "What about it?"

"Do you have any ideas?"

"One or two," he answered, lifting a dark strand of damp hair from her cheek.

"Great!"

"Ideas don't write themselves, so don't get too excited," he warned.

She looked at him curiously. "You do plan to write a song for me, don't you? You didn't ask me here just so you could torture me for wrecking your car?"

He didn't give her a direct answer, which told her a lot. "I can't write if I'm blocked. I told you that coming in."

"But writer's block can be broken, the same as batting slumps and bad luck."

"We'll see."

"Try to work up a little enthusiasm. I don't want just any old song, you know. My whole career might be riding on the song you write for me."

"I never write just any old song," he said tersely. "I write songs to touch people. I write songs I expect will be around for a long time because they mean something—to others as well as myself."

Chelsea smiled. She'd pricked his ego. Maybe that was the key to unblocking him.

DAKOTA WAS RIGHT.

He didn't write lame songs.

Chelsea sat in the audience at Dakota Country that evening, listening to him perform, and thought it was no wonder he had sponsors lining up at the door to underwrite his concerts. She was amazed a blue-jeans company hadn't seen the windfall his endorsement would bring. It ought to be illegal to wear jeans that tight . . . and probably was.

The ballad he was singing was an emotional minefield, and the audience was totally caught up in it. She had made the right decision; Dakota was a genius. When he finished the song, she and every member of the audience was drained, wrung out, content.

But Chelsea wanted something different. The song she wanted Dakota to write for her had to be uplifting and optimistic.

Like her.

Despite a childhood that would be fodder for a half-dozen or so movies-of-the-week, Chelsea had refused to be a victim. She believed that if you let the bad things that happened to you in life control the rest of your life, then you lost. It was how people reacted to what happened to them that decided who won and who lost.

Winning was not giving in, not accepting a life or a fate you didn't want. It was fighting back, going on—surviving.

"I'd like to get someone in the audience to come up onstage and sing a song for us. Ladies and gentlemen, give a big round of encouragement to Chelsea Stone!"

Chelsea heard her name and then everyone started clapping.

She was going to kill Dakota Law—right after he wrote her a song. But at the moment she had no choice but to go onstage and act like they were friends. He'd put her on the spot and in the spotlight.

The crowd's enthusiasm and anticipation were both scary and exciting. She'd never suffered from stage fright, but then she'd sung before rock audiences who knew what they were getting. This audience wanted country music. What would they think of her?

Would they accept her or boo her off the stage?

Surely, with Dakota there, they would give her a chance.

"What am I supposed to sing?" she whispered to Dakota when she reached the stage.

"Whatever you want. Here's your chance to try out a country-music audience and see how you like it. Don't freak. It's only a small club. Just pick out a song and go for it."

The audience had quieted and waited expectantly.

Chelsea could feel her heart pounding. She wasn't prepared. It was warm. She felt dizzy.

She couldn't do it.

Oh, yes, you can, a voice from her childhood insisted. And she listened to that voice—the voice that had never failed her. The voice that had gotten her through the emotional and physical cruelty. The voice that told her never to show fear.

She didn't know where she found the nerve or the presence of mind, but she launched into a parody of "Kentucky Woman," only she sang it as "Dakota's Women."

She was relying on humor and good fun. It wasn't a real test of whether or not country-music fans would accept her, but it was ever so much better than a kick in the stomach.

Somehow she got through the song.

The rest of the evening and the ride home went by in a daze for Chelsea. The full reality of how much of a risk she was taking had sunk in when she'd performed without her accepting fans and a backlog of hits to support her.

"You haven't said a word since we left the club," Dakota remarked, as they pulled into the long winding drive to his home.

"I'm thinking," she explained.

"About what?"

"Where the gardener keeps the rat poison," she joked, hiding her doubts and fears.

"Aw, come on, I thought you'd enjoy it. Besides, the audience loved you. And I'm the one who ought to be sore about that 'Dakota's Women' bit you sang."

"You deserved it," she said, stifling a smile.

He came around to let her out of the car, ever the gentleman.

She followed him to the front door.

As he was putting his key in the lock, he asked, "Are you hungry? I can have the cook make us a snack if you want."

"No, I'm too keyed up to be hungry."

"In that case we could play tennis...."

"No," she said. "What is it with you, today? Why are you so bent on embarrassing me?"

"I'm just doing my job," he said, standing aside after he'd opened the door.

"What are you talking about?" she asked, as he followed her into the house.

"I'm observing you in order to write a song for you. Isn't that what you wanted? Oh, look— someone's sent me flowers," he said, going to the vase of fresh tulips on the round table in the foyer.

Dakota reached for the tiny envelope tucked in amid the flowers. He slipped the card out and read aloud.

"Happy Birthday!
Love, Me"

A look of puzzlement crossed his face. "There's obviously been some sort of mix-up. My birthday isn't for months."

"What time is it?" Chelsea leaned over to smell the white tulips.

"What time is it?"

She nodded.

He glanced at his watch. "Twelve-thirty, why?"

"Because as of midnight, it's my birthday. The flowers are for me, not you."

"Why didn't you tell me it was your birthday? I would have ordered champagne and a birthday cake at the club to celebrate."

"My birthday just started at midnight, somewhere on the ride home," she said with a shrug.

"So how old are you?"

"That's none of your business."

"Sure, it is. I have to know to get the spankings right."

She didn't like the look in his eyes, and began inching away. "You wouldn't dare...."

He pushed back his cowboy hat, smiled wickedly, and took the three long-legged steps necessary to tug her up against the lean, hard line of his body.

"Dakota, what ... what do you think you're doing?"

He answered her by slowly tracing her pouty bottom lip with his thumb. "I figured since Tucker took care of the flowers, I'd take care of the birthday kiss."

"That's really not—" she began.

"It's the gentlemanly thing to do," he insisted. He winked, then added, "And you know me, I'm always a gentleman."

"Dakota, please..." She giggled nervously.

"Aw, you don't have to beg, precious...."

Before she could reply, he lowered his lips to hers, which were parted in surprise.

The kiss started as a nibble, then built.

Chelsea could feel the beating of his heart and smell his cologne. His eyes were closed and she noticed how thick his lashes were. Her eyes were open; that was the way she went through life.

Fleetingly, she wondered what he was thinking, then she was lost in a whirlpool of sensations that carried her into murky waters.

"Happy Birthday, Chelsea," Dakota said, his voice husky with passion.

Then the devilment returned to his eyes. "Now, about that spanking . . ." he began.

"Ouch, woman! You've got to learn to stop doing that," he exclaimed, rubbing his arm where she'd punched him.

6

DAKOTA SWORE AS HE stuck a piece of tissue on his face where he'd nicked his chin with his razor. The tissue joined three other bits, making his face look like a first grader's art project.

He was distracted, had been distracted, ever since Chelsea Stone had waltzed into—actually *crashed* was a better word—into his life.

Six months ago she'd turned his career upside down. Now she was making him reconsider his life.

He'd been singing about love, but he'd never felt the emotion. He wrote love songs with his head, not his heart. Was his writer's block forcing him to think about what was missing in his life?

All he knew was that he didn't believe in love and he felt like a fake writing about it.

How could he be attracted to Chelsea Stone?

He didn't approve of her.

Not of the way she dressed. Nor her attitude. Nor her life-style, and especially not of her relationship with Tucker Gable. Why, the two of them practically made love onstage when they performed together at rock concerts. They were incendiary in front of a crowd, almost setting the audience on fire.

No. Chelsea Stone was not the woman for him.

He liked the sort of girls he'd grown up around. Women who wore gloves, white ones—not black net. Women who spoke softly—not in a voice more gravelly than his own. Women who knew how to behave themselves—not women who . . . who challenged him?

Was that true?

No. Chelsea Stone wasn't right for him, but it wasn't because she challenged him. It was because she was involved with Tucker Gable. It was dangerous to let this infatuation he felt for her develop.

Still, she and Tucker weren't *married*. Didn't that make her fair game romantically? Maybe. But pursuing Chelsea was doomed to end badly.

He told his reflection that he was only taking her out dancing to celebrate her birthday. That it had nothing to do with the way she kissed. That spending time with her was the only way to get himself unblocked.

Then, once he was able to write again, he'd give her the song she wanted. Write her out of his life.

Satisfied he'd reached a sensible decision, Dakota peeled the bits of tissue off his face and finished getting dressed.

He was opening a bottle of champagne when Chelsea came downstairs to join him. It was clear that white gloves had never entered her mind.

"Don't you have something to wear that isn't see-through?" he demanded, observing the sheer black blouse that laced up the front with a black satin ribbon. She wore a frilly black bra under it, but somehow it made the outfit even more indecent.

"Why, I don't have anything to hide," she answered, as she slid a silver-studded black belt through the loops of her tight, button-fly jeans.

To keep himself from staring, Dakota poured her a glass of champagne and handed it to her.

"Aren't you going to make a birthday toast?" She eyed his empty glass.

"Of course." He poured champagne into his glass, then turned to face her and tried not to look at the crests of her breasts swelling over the black lace bra. The sheer black fabric of the blouse only made them more inviting.

"To, ah . . ."

"Don't tell me your block extends to toasts, as well. Come on, the bubbles will all disappear if you don't come up with something soon."

"Ah . . ."

"You said that already."

"To making better decisions," he blurted out. He lifted his glass and tossed down its contents.

"What's that supposed to mean?" she asked, after sipping her champagne.

"Whatever you want it to. You could choose better music, better men . . . a better blouse."

"Will you chill about the blouse. There's nothing wrong with it. Tucker likes it," she added defiantly.

"Oh, well. You should have told me. If Tucker likes it, then by all means—"

"Could we just go?" Chelsea set her champagne glass on the table with a toss of her long dark curls.

"Of course." He'd made her angry again. What was wrong with him? His mother would be appalled at his lack of manners around a lady. But then, Chelsea Stone wasn't a lady, he was reminded, as he followed her to the car, watching the sway of her hips. Jeans did the same thing for her long legs as short skirts. Wasn't there something she didn't look good in? he wondered, as he held the door for her to slide into the soft bucket seat.

The scent of her perfume drifted up to tease him when he bent to close the car door. He wondered just when it had been that he'd become suicidal. Had it been six months ago—or just lately?

As they headed down the long drive, he saw her take out her lipstick and gloss her full lips with her signature scarlet hue. The atmosphere in the car was slightly tense, so he suggested turning on the radio.

He hadn't really wanted to ruin her birthday. Maybe some music would put them both in a more festive mood.

But she stayed his hand when he reached for the controls. "No, let's talk."

"About what?"

"About the kind of song I want you to write for me. I want a special song. A song so special that no one else can sing it. A song about . . ."

He waited, but she didn't finish the sentence. She shivered violently and stared out the car window into the lengthening shadows of dusk.

"What's wrong?" he asked, looking over at her.

"I don't know. I just got a chill. It's probably nothing. This song is so important to me that I can't bear to think you won't be able to write it."

"I'm doing my best, but nothing's coming."

"Nothing?"

"Nothing worth putting down on paper."

"How do you know? Maybe . . ."

"No, I know. It has to feel right. It has to haunt you." He swore at a big rig that flew past them recklessly.

"How do you get your ideas for a song?"

"I read a lot."

"You read?" she echoed with unflattering disbelief. "Like what?"

"Everything. I read fiction, newspapers and magazines. And I listen to talk shows on the radio and television. You need input for output."

She turned toward him in her seat. "I don't understand how reading and watching television help you to write songs."

Pulling onto the highway, Dakota explained. "They help to fill my mind with images of the times and culture we live in. And stories set in the past are full of myth and legend I interpret for modern times. Newspapers are great for odd turns of speech. Songwriting is a lot of little details and observations put together around a theme."

"So a song just doesn't come to you, then. You set out deliberately to write it, to deliver a certain message in the lyrics."

Dakota shook his head. "No, it's both. Sometimes, actually often, a phrase will come to me full-blown out of the blue."

"But nothing's come to you in the past six months...."

"A phrase doesn't make a song, Chelsea. I've got lots of phrases."

"Where?"

"In my computer. I used to write them down on whatever was handy, but I kept losing the bits of paper, so now I keep the phrases I come up with stored in a file in my computer."

"What you're really telling me is that you write with your head and not your heart. Is that right, Dakota?"

He didn't answer her.

Instead he stared at the road, looking for the exit that would take them to the Whiskey River honky-tonk, and wondering how she had discovered that in one conversation.

She had him wondering whether, if he changed the process and started writing from the heart, his career might disappear. The one truism everyone in the entertainment business knew was: Don't mess with what works for you.

But who was he kidding? At the moment, nothing was working for him.

"What about melodies?" Chelsea asked, shifting the conversation from words to music. "Do you write those with your head or your heart?"

Dakota didn't answer immediately. "I haven't the foggiest idea," he finally said. "I imagine you might say both as the melodies just seem to pop into my head."

"You mean you don't work them out on an instrument? Surely not?"

"No instrument. I don't have that kind of patience. Besides, I find I get more original melodies without trial and error on an instrument where I'm sure I'd tend to repeat old patterns."

"So which do you get first, the lyrics or the melody?"

"Why are you so curious about the way I write songs? No one else has ever asked me all these questions. I just show them the song once I've written it."

"I told you. I want a special song. I want to have 'input'."

"I don't cowrite." He knew his words were cold, but he couldn't help it. He didn't like allowing anyone access to his thoughts, his feelings.

"I don't want to cowrite the song with you. I'm not a writer."

"Then I don't get it," he said, sounding puzzled as they turned off the highway into the parking lot of the Whiskey River honky-tonk. "What are you talking about when you say you want input?" He stopped the car, parked and turned to her, waiting for her answer.

"By input I mean I want you to get to know me, to know how I feel, who I am."

"Then let's do it." He opened the car door. The music from the honky-tonk spilled into the car. "Do you know how to do the reggae cowboy?"

She shook her head no.

"The tush push?"

"What!"

"The country two-step?" he finally said.

"That sounds like something I can handle."

"And here I was sure you'd go for the tush push. See, I'm getting to know you better already," he said, with a wink, as they got out of the car.

"Wait a minute," Chelsea said.

"Why? What's wrong?"

"Nothing. I just want you to show me the two-step before we go inside. I don't want to be embarrassed in front of . . . Well, you know, in case anyone recognizes me."

"Okay," he agreed, seeing that she really was nervous. He reached inside the car, hunted up a CD disc that had a song with eighty-five to ninety-five beats a minute, and inserted it in the player.

"You don't really have to know the steps," he explained, taking her into his arms. "Lots of people just improvise." And then he proceeded to do just that because he hadn't the faintest idea how to do the two-step.

Before long, she caught on to that fact.

When he stepped on her boot for about the sixth time, Chelsea socked him in the arm. "Dakota Law, you're nothing but a fraud. Why, you don't know nuthin' 'bout dancin' no two-step. Admit it."

"I never said I did. I asked you if you did," he said, unrepentant. "All I wanted to do was show you a good time on your birthday."

The CD player stopped, and they heard the band inside the honky-tonk rev up their version of "Boot Scootin' Boogie."

"We can leave if you want to," Dakota offered.

"No, I want to go inside and watch the dancers," Chelsea insisted.

"Then let's do it." He reached into the back seat for his white Stetson and jammed it on his head.

"I wish I had one of those to hide under," Chelsea said wistfully as they entered the club and found themselves awash in a sea of denim, fringe, neon, and flashing lights.

She turned toward the dance floor where a crowd of spectators swarmed around the wooden railing.

"Just a sec," Dakota said, steering her toward a small store set up inside the dance club.

She looked puzzled until he instructed the clerk to hand over a black cowboy hat for her. "Now maybe we can be incognito," he said, paying the clerk.

When Dakota had finally elbowed them through the crowd to a good spot at the railing by the dance floor, he asked what she wanted to drink.

"Well, since I'm in your backyard, I guess I'll try a mint julep." At the look of surprise on his face, Chelsea quipped, "Unless you'd rather I order my regular drink."

"Your regular drink . . . ?"

Not wanting to disappoint him, she played to her bad-girl image. "Yeah, you know—a screaming orgasm."

"A mint julep it is." He ducked away quickly into the crowd, but not before she'd seen him blush.

Chelsea turned her attention to the dance floor where it looked like at least five hundred people were dancing to the Neon Cactus band. The band's singer was a petite blonde in a red sequined dress and feather earrings. Watching her made Chelsea long to be onstage. There was nothing like the rush she felt from the applause of the crowd.

It was the only time she really felt loved.

She missed the times onstage with Tucker. Dear Tucker, what would she do without him in her life?

Dakota returned with a cold long-neck beer for him and a highball glass for her.

He chugged his beer while she took a tentative sip of her drink. She made a face and looked at her drink more closely. "There's a Maraschino cherry in a mint julep?"

"They were out of mint leaves," Dakota explained. "So I got you a blackberry collins. It's what Melinda, my assistant, drinks. She was at the bar and suggested it."

"What you're saying is you were too chicken to order me a screaming orgasm," she taunted.

"No," he countered, his blue eyes meeting hers in a contest of wills. "What I'm saying is I never order a screaming orgasm, I only serve them."

"Oh," was all she said.

They stood at the railing watching the intricate footwork, spins and turns of the line dancers. The music was upbeat and the spirit of fun on the dance floor was infectious.

So much so that when the band moved to the new hit ballad, "She Left Me and It Wasn't Even Rainin,'" Dakota leaned forward and whispered, "You want to dance?"

It was more a dare than a request, Chelsea thought, considering his dancing ability. She looked over her shoulder to see if he was teasing or serious. "Sure you don't mind being seen with me?" she asked, remembering his disapproval of her attire.

"Are you kidding? With you wearing that see-through blouse, no one's seen me yet—or is likely to." He placed his hand in the center of her back, urging her to join him on the dance floor.

When Dakota pulled her into his arms, he didn't even attempt the country two-step. Instead, he showed a fluid smoothness—evidence that he'd attended his share of debutante balls before leaving home.

Chelsea counted it lucky that no one had recognized either of them in the crowded honky-tonk. They'd blended in with the others wearing denim and cowboy hats—and she'd seen a few outfits that had made even her sheer blouse look tame.

She let herself be swept up into the romantic mood. Allowed herself to pretend she was having the perfect birthday evening. Dakota's arms held her in a tight embrace while he nuzzled his chin alongside her forehead. The heat of his body released the spicy scent of his cologne and worked its sensual magic.

She was drifting along in a romantic trance when she felt someone tap her on the shoulder. At first she thought it was Dakota, but then she heard an impatient feminine voice say, "I'm cutting in."

Chelsea lifted her head from Dakota's shoulder and turned to see Melinda Jackson gazing proprietarily at Dakota. She was dressed to kill in a pair of pressed jeans, red fringed jacket and matching red cowboy hat and boots.

Chelsea pulled out of Dakota's embrace and left him to his assistant. As she headed toward the bar for a long-neck beer, she looked back over her shoulder and saw that Melinda had plastered herself to her boss as close as a coat of paint. Melinda's smile was victorious as she looked at Chelsea over Dakota's shoulder.

Since Dakota's back was to Chelsea she couldn't tell if he was annoyed or pleased about the change in partners, but she would have bet on the latter.

Chelsea went to the end of the bar where the female bartender was sitting on a stool enjoying the lull while the dance floor was full because of the slow dance. Chelsea placed her order for a long-neck, then reached into her jeans pocket for change when the bartender set the cold bottle of beer down before her.

"Your money isn't good here, Miss Stone."

Chelsea's head snapped up to look at the red-headed bartender, who smiled at her, then went on to explain, "I recognized you and Dakota when you came in. I'm a big fan. Of both of you."

"Uh . . . thanks. Does Dakota come in here a lot, then?" Chelsea asked, taking a swallow of beer to cool her throat, which was dry from the smoky club.

"No. Never been here that I know of. I stood in line for tickets to his last big concert and believe me, the show was worth every penny. He's major. And so are you, of course."

"Does she come in here often?" Chelsea nodded at Melinda Jackson.

"You mean the one in red?" the bartender asked. Chelsea nodded.

"No, can't say as I've seen her before. Looks like she knows him, though. Pretty well."

"Yeah." Chelsea sighed.

The song ended and the band announced a twenty-minute break.

Chelsea watched as Melinda tugged Dakota's arm to get his attention, then engaged him in conversation. He bent his head to listen intently to what she was saying. Chelsea would have bet money that Melinda was the type of woman who put on a whispery little-girl voice and played to a man's ego.

When the two of them finally drifted toward the bar with the crowd, Chelsea tossed back the last of her beer . . . and felt in the mood for another one.

The suddenly busy bartender rushed to fill the orders called out from the jostling crowd. A cowboy with an earring bumped into Chelsea. He squinted down at her. "Hey, you're Chelsea St—"

"We were just leaving," Dakota interrupted, silencing the cowboy with a steely gaze.

The cowboy seemed about to challenge Dakota when a look of recognition dawned on his face. "Oh, sure thing. Sorry to bother you, man."

Dakota took Chelsea's elbow and began to steer her out of the club.

"Will you quit," she objected, trying to twist free. "I wanted another beer."

When he wouldn't let go but kept determinedly propelling her toward the door, she snapped, "What cave did you crawl out of? Don't you know women aren't dragged around anymore? Let go of me."

Dakota didn't release his firm grip on her arm until they were outside the club.

"Listen," he said as she rubbed her elbow angrily, "I didn't think you'd want to spend your birthday evening signing autographs until dawn. In case you weren't listening, that guy with the earring was about to announce your presence to the entire club."

"You're right, it was time to leave," Chelsea admitted, feeling a bit embarrassed. But she didn't apologize. After all, he had left her to fend for herself at the bar while his butter-wouldn't-melt-in-her-mouth assistant built up his ego. *Men.*

"Are you hungry?" he asked, hoping food would put her in a better mood.

"I don't suppose you have any good Chinese restaurants in Nashville . . ." she began poutily.

"Since it's your birthday, we could look," he answered, which was a far more generous response than she deserved, she knew.

"No, I'm tired. Let's just go home."

"Your coach, madame," he said when they reached the car. "I'll have you home by midnight so you can keep your glass slipper."

Chelsea rolled her eyes. "No princess in her right mind would ever do the country two-step with you in glass slippers."

"That's why I don't make it a practice of dancing with princesses," he said, closing the car door.

The next thing she knew they were home and Dakota was trying to wake her.

"You're not much of a wild woman, Chelsea Stone," he said as he carried her into the house in his arms like a sleepy child.

"What do you mean?" she asked on a wide yawn.

"I mean one blackberry collins and a beer chaser and you're out like a light. You snored all the way home. I almost thought I had Pokey sleeping on the seat beside me, you were so noisy."

"I was not," she objected strenuously. "I do not snore."

"Tucker tell you that, too?"

She ignored his remark and demanded to be put down at once.

"Come on out to the kitchen for a minute," he coaxed, when she would have gone upstairs to bed.

"Why?"

"Just come, okay?"

She shrugged, and followed him out to the kitchen.

When they entered the kitchen, Dakota went straight to the refrigerator. Pokey, who had been asleep on a mat under the table, yawned and got up slowly.

"You're a great watchdog," Dakota said as the Lab ambled over to stand beside him, wagging her tail hopefully.

Opening the refrigerator, Dakota took out a piece of ham and threw it to Pokey to keep her busy. Then, humming "Happy Birthday to You," he withdrew a beautifully frosted birthday cake with candles already on top, just waiting to be lit.

Chelsea squealed with delight. "Where did that come from?" she asked, with surprise. "It's beautiful."

"I had the cook make it before he left. I hope you like chocolate cake."

"Even better than Chinese food. Where are the plates?"

"Don't be in such a hurry," he said, setting the cake on the counter. "First we have to light the candles so you can make a wish and blow them out."

When he had the cake blazing, Chelsea took a deep breath and blew out all the candles on the first try.

"I guess I don't have to ask what you wished for, do I?" Dakota said, as she picked off the melting candles while he got them plates and forks.

"Nope. A hit song, of course. And since I blew out the candles with one breath, I'm sure to get my wish."

She bit into her generous slice of cake. "Mmm." She sighed. "This is delicious."

Pokey barked, begging for her own slice.

"No, dogs can't have chocolate," Dakota scolded.

Pokey barked again, as if to say, "What about the vanilla frosting?"

Chelsea laughed and gave her a generous dollop from her plate.

"Seconds?" Dakota asked, after Chelsea had polished off her piece.

She shook her head no. "Thanks, Dakota, for trying to make my birthday special." She got up and came around the counter to kiss his cheek. "I'm going to bed."

"Not just yet," he said, holding her wrist.

"Why not?"

"We've got your birthday dance to finish," he explained. He turned on the radio and fiddled with the buttons until he found a slow song, Vince Gill's beautiful "I Still Believe in You."

Pokey cocked her head and watched the two of them slow dancing around the kitchen.

"Now this is more like it," Chelsea said dreamily, listening to the words to the song.

"I didn't know you cared." Dakota lowered her into a sexy dip.

"No, I mean the song. The words are so personal. You can tell how special they are to him when he sings the song. I don't think any other singer could do it as well. It's his song. That's the kind of song I want you to write for me."

"You don't want much, do you?" Dakota asked, bringing her back up from the dip. They continued dancing, lost in the beautiful lyrics of the song.

And the moment.

Their dreamy state was shattered when the disc jockey interrupted the song with a special bulletin.

"This just in. Rock star Tucker Gable's tour bus was involved in an accident after leaving Iowa for a performance at the Riverport Theater in St. Louis. The bus carrying all the band members was on a bridge that collapsed into the raging floodwaters that have been plaguing the Midwest. All the band members have been rescued except Tucker Gable. He is still listed as missing. We'll bring you more news of this possible tragedy when we have it."

Her face ashen, Chelsea collapsed in Dakota's arms with a keening wail of disbelief.

7

DAKOTA'S ARMS WERE numb, but he didn't dare move.

If he moved, he'd wake Chelsea. He'd held her for hours and she'd finally fallen asleep in his arms. She'd clung to him, desperate to believe his reassurances that Tucker would be found.

That he'd be alive.

That he'd be all right.

He hoped to God it was true, but in his heart he was afraid the morning light would bring Chelsea's worst nightmare. Dakota didn't think there was much hope that Tucker would even be found, much less still be alive. He'd spent the sleepless night wondering how he was going to tell Chelsea the brutal truth.

She was so strong and resilient, so fiercely independent, that Dakota had been stunned at her sudden vulnerability, at her wild grief and abject despair when she'd heard the news bulletin.

Chelsea moaned in her sleep, and called out Tucker's name in a frightened whimper.

Dakota stroked her, and murmured soothing words to comfort her. When she quieted, he looked down at her beautiful face composed in restless slumber and wondered what it would feel like to have someone love him, care about him like that. Tucker was one lucky son of a bitch—if he was alive.

Dakota had left the radio on and had listened to the bulletins throughout the night, but there had been no new information. Tucker was still missing. Night was the enemy. The streaks of dawn Dakota could see filtering through the curtain would bring more news.

Pokey, who seemed to know something was wrong, lay on the floor beside Dakota's chair, keeping the lonely vigil with him.

Dakota knew that when Chelsea woke she'd want to fly to St. Louis to see the rest of the band, to talk to the members about Tucker. He'd managed to keep her from doing it last night by telling her over and over there was nothing anyone could do till morning.

The song on the radio drifted into his consciousness. It was the Vince Gill song that he and Chelsea had been dancing to last night.

Last night when there had been such possibilities.

It seemed like an eternity ago.

The phone rang then; its shrill noise in the silent morning startled Dakota and made Pokey bark.

"Tucker!" Chelsea's eyes were wild and filled with hope as she came awake.

"Chelsea, please, it's probably a reporter who's gotten wind that you're here. You'd better let me get it."

But she wasn't listening. She crawled off his lap and raced for the phone.

"Tucker!" she cried into the receiver as she picked up the phone.

Dakota waited for her to sag with disappointment. He got up to catch her if need be, to hold her as she cried.

"It is Tucker! I told you," she called to Dakota, her voice filled with relief and excitement. "He's alive. I knew you were alive, you had to be alive! Oh, my God, Tucker I was so scared—"

"Scared? Why were you scared? I promised you I'd get there in one piece," Tucker replied, his voice weak.

"I know, but when I heard the bulletin that you were missing in the river... Oh, Tucker..." She started to cry.

Dakota put his arm around her and she sniffled while Tucker reassured her that he was fine. By

some miracle he'd managed to hold on to a floating log throughout the night. He'd been spotted just
after daybreak and picked up by a helicopter
search-and-rescue team.

"Tucker, I was so afraid I'd lost you. I couldn't
stand it if . . ." Chelsea sobbed.

"Babe, please don't cry. . . ."

"Oh, Tucker, I got this . . . this chill last night, this
awful feeling around eight o'clock when Dakota
and I were in the car on the way to Whiskey River.
That must have been about the time your bus . . .
you went off the bridge. Dammit, Tucker, you
promised you'd be careful. And that you'd call me
when you got to the Riverport Theater—"

"But I never got to the Riverport Theater, babe."

"Where are you? You are all right, aren't you?"
she demanded, alarm creeping into her voice.

"I'm pretty all right."

"What in the hell does that mean, Tucker. What
aren't you telling me? What's wrong?"

"Calm down, babe. It's nothing, really. I'm just
damn lucky to even be alive. I've got this little broken leg, is all."

"I'm coming there," she told him.

"You can't. What about your song?"

"I'll put it on hold for the time being. I'll come get
you and nurse you back to health."

Dakota didn't want her to go and the offer he made was based on that fact more than Southern hospitality. "He can stay here," he heard himself say. "There's plenty of room, and we can continue to work on the song for you while Tucker recuperates."

Chelsea turned back to the phone and relayed Dakota's offer.

"Are you sure that's a good idea, babe?"

"I'm sure. I'll catch a flight and fetch you back here."

"That's not necessary. I'm going to be released today after they put on a cast. Just meet me at the airport, okay?"

"I can't wait to see you, Tucker," she said, her voice soft with emotion.

Chelsea hung up the phone, oblivious to the fact that Dakota wasn't nearly as thrilled as she was about the impending arrival of Tucker Gable.

TUCKER GABLE'S ARRIVAL was anything but quiet.

An army of reporters followed his limo from the airport and shoved microphones at him as he was assisted into Dakota's house.

Everyone wanted to know about his harrowing accident and the night spent in the raging floodwaters, and why he was staying with Dakota Law.

He had no comment for all questions.

And through it all Chelsea dithered, giddy as a child at Christmas, wearing her relief that Tucker was okay like a warm cloak.

The band members who'd come along for the ride joked and tormented Tucker and signed his cast with sundry obscene sentiments. With their long hair and ear studs, tattered jeans and leather jackets, they struck an incongruous note in Dakota's wood-paneled library filled with books and antiques.

Dakota stayed on the sidelines watching Tucker and Chelsea interact, and said little. It was impossible to miss the fact that she couldn't seem to keep her hands off Tucker.

As the morning progressed, Dakota got even quieter.

Finally, after the band members departed and Tucker was settled on the sofa with his foot propped up to keep his leg from swelling beneath his cast, Dakota excused himself to take care of some business.

"Will you *please* light somewhere," Tucker said to Chelsea when the two of them were alone. "You keep flitting around like a drunken moth. I want to hear all about how things are going with you."

"Are you sure I can't get you something?" she asked, hovering anxiously. "Are you thirsty? I could have the cook make you some tea. Do you need a pillow?"

"I'm fine, babe. Now sit and talk."

Chelsea gave in and flopped down in an oversize leather wing chair. "What do you want to know?"

"I want to know how the songwriting is going."

"It's not," Chelsea said, sighing. "Dakota is still blocked."

"My moving into his house probably isn't going to help matters. Are you sure he invited me? Or is this one of your 'take no prisoners' schemes?" Tucker's voice was filled with suspicion.

"Don't be silly. Of course, he invited you."

"*Chel-sea . . .*"

"He *did* invite you. After I said I was leaving to go and get you and look after you. Are you satisfied?"

"Well, I expect you railroaded him into letting me stay here. That's why he was so quiet all morning."

"Shut up, Cheesebrain. Now that you're here, you've got to help me figure out a way to get Dakota unblocked so he writes me a song. Time is running out. If I don't have a hit song out soon, people are going to forget who I am. I'll be an eighties has-been."

"Don't go getting all paranoid on me. Your career is far from over. Didn't you pay any attention at all to the response you got at Farm Aid? The crowd went wild when you sang."

"Yeah, but that was all old material. I can't go on trading on my old stuff—I can't even go on singing it, because I risk damaging my vocal chords."

"Look, it's not that complicated, babe. If Dakota can't get it together to write you a song, then we'll find someone else to write you a hit. He's not the only songwriter in the world, you know."

"No," Chelsea objected, her chin tilted in determination. "It's got to be Dakota."

"Why?" Tucker groaned as he tried to adjust his leg to a more comfortable position.

"Do you need some more pain medication?" Chelsea rose from her chair to fetch some.

"No. I'm fine. Just answer my question. Why does it have to be Dakota?"

"Because...because..." She began pacing, then stopped to fiddle with a flower arrangement on the credenza behind Dakota's desk. "Look, don't tell him this, but it's because I love his songs."

"Why would you not want him to know that?"

"I don't know. I just don't, okay?"

"Are you sure it's not because you really do feel responsible for Dakota's not being able to write?

That you feel guilty about wrecking his car and all?"

"I don't know. Maybe," she admitted reluctantly. Whatever the cause, she just knew she didn't want to explore why she felt the way she did.

Tucker rubbed his chin with his forefinger, thoughtfully. "Because if that is the reason, I think maybe I've got an idea that might help."

"Really?" Chelsea gave him her full attention.

At that moment the door to the library opened and a black blur shot across the room.

"What in the Sam Hell—?" Tucker leaned back and braced himself.

"No, Pokey. Down. Come here."

"They let horses in the house in the South?" Tucker asked, as Chelsea allowed the huge dog to rest her big black paws on her shoulders and lick her face.

"No, Cheesebrain. This is Pokey. She's Dakota's puppy."

"That's no puppy. That thing weighs at least one hundred pounds."

"Shh . . . you'll hurt her feelings. She thinks she's a lapdog."

"Just as long as it's not my lap she wants to sit on."

Pokey looked over at Tucker, dismissed him as no threat, and plopped down on the hardwood floor beside Chelsea's chair.

"Now, about your idea..." Chelsea said, returning to their interrupted conversation.

DAKOTA WAS DEEP IN thought as he flew home from Branson, Missouri. He'd spent the afternoon getting a feel for what was happening in the booming town that was becoming known as the new Nashville. Dozens of country-music stars were building their own theaters in Branson and the fans were flocking to their shows by the thousands.

It was a great setup for those stars who were weary of touring. And for the star who wanted to spend more time at home, start a family...

A family.

Since his own had shunned him, he'd tried not to think about the concept. It was too painful.

Not that there weren't any good memories; there were.

There just weren't any warm ones.

Affection might have been felt, but it had never been shown. In his family, the emphasis had been on appearances. In banking it was important that your standing in the community be maintained. There could never be the slightest hint of scandal. Any impropriety in your personal life could be construed as a weakness that might bleed over into your professional life.

That was bad enough, but perhaps even worse was his mother's drive to be at the top of society in their community—a closed society that dictated manners and opinions, and measured personal worth according to family background and professional status.

His mother hadn't objected to the fact that he'd wanted a career in music; only that it wasn't in the opera or with a symphony.

Was it getting older that made him long for what he didn't have? And premature senility that had him thinking about marriage to Chelsea Stone—a completely unsuitable woman, who was involved with another man.

It was madness.

She was all wrong for him.

Unfortunately, he was afraid he was falling in love with her.

After stopping by his record company's offices on Music Circle to reassure them he was working on the album, and to check on the schedule for making the music video for launching the first single from the album, he headed home.

He felt a little like he suspected a new husband might when the old husband turned out not to be dead after all. At least his dog loved him. Pokey met him at the door, her tail thumping with eager delight.

"You been guarding the silverware, girl?" Dakota grumbled. He scratched the playful dog behind the ears, then bent to rub her belly while she squirmed with absolute bliss.

"Where is everyone?" he wondered aloud when he got to his feet and loosened his tie. Pokey followed him down the hall to the library, but they found it deserted.

Chelsea and Tucker were probably out in the kitchen as it was the cook's day off. Chelsea was no doubt hovering over him, feeding him broth and crackers.

But they weren't in the kitchen, either. They couldn't have gone far, he surmised. Tucker needed to stay off his leg for a few days, anyway.

Back out in the hall, he heard laughter floating down the stairs.

He followed the sound to Chelsea's bedroom.

The door was open.

Dakota walked inside and Pokey followed, hopped up on the unmade bed and sprawled across it.

He heard the water running in the adjoining bath. Maybe he'd imagined hearing laughter. Perhaps it had been Chelsea in the shower singing that he'd heard. It wouldn't do for her to come out of the shower and find him snooping in her bedroom.

He turned to leave, then stopped dead in his tracks.

"Oww . . . Tucker Gable, I swear that cast is a lethal weapon."

"The better to protect you with, my dear. I told you you were always safe with me." Tucker laughed, then added, "I don't think this bathtub was meant for two. We're going to have to be careful I don't wind up breaking my other leg."

Dakota didn't wait to hear anymore.

He left the room feeling like a fool.

He'd almost talked himself into believing there wasn't anything more between Chelsea and Tucker than a strong friendship. Anyone, but a fool like himself, could see they were lovers.

He had to work through his block.

As it stood, he couldn't ask them to leave. What would he say? That he was falling in love with Chelsea?

Hardly.

But if he wrote her a song, she would take it and go. He'd be rid of both of them.

Yes, that was what he wanted, he told himself.

He wanted to be alone.

THE NEXT MORNING Dakota left early with the excuse of a business breakfast appointment. It was a lie, but he couldn't face sitting and watching Chelsea and Tucker flirting outrageously, as was their habit.

He frittered away the day playing tourist, eavesdropping on the other tourists visiting the museums, souvenir shops and showcases on Demon Breu Street. All it did was make him appreciate how much country music was loved. It didn't inspire the song he'd hoped for.

He almost went to the Opryland Theme Park, but decided he was likely to be recognized. Instead, he headed for Tootsie's Orchid Lounge and enough beer to get seriously mellow.

That didn't work, either. Still no song idea came to him. So he took himself home. On the drive up to the house he saw a tennis ball lying in the flower bed where Pokey must have dropped it. She loved playing catch with the gardener.

And he'd loved playing tennis with Chelsea.

That was something Tucker couldn't do with his broken leg. Dakota was in a much better mood as he went inside to hunt up Chelsea for a game of tennis.

A quick check of the downstairs yielded no sign of her. The house was quiet. The cook lived on the premises in the carriage house, and the gardener had gone home.

He stopped to listen carefully, but no strains of laughter floated down the stairs.

"Pokey, where are you, girl?" he called out.

A quiet bark seemed to come from upstairs. Dakota took the steps two at a time. He checked his own bedroom first, but no Pokey.

The door to Chelsea's room was ajar and he was drawn to it irresistibly. He took a deep breath before he pushed it open, afraid of what he might see.

There was someone in Chelsea's unmade bed, all right.

Pokey was sprawled there, happily chewing on one of Chelsea's new leather cowboy boots.

"Pokey! Bad girl," Dakota admonished, taking the boot from her, but the damage had already been done.

Dakota picked up the boot and its mate to stow them in the closet where, he thought peevishly, they should have been in the first place.

As he passed the large mirrored dresser he saw a bright scrap of lingerie nestled in the white tissue folds of an open white gift box. He set the boots down and picked up the bit of silk—a sheer red teddy with a thong back—and let it dangle from his fingertip as if it were a piece of evidence from a crime that had been committed.

Chelsea's image—a cloud of dark curls, red lips and long legs—flashed in his mind. The teddy would cling to every curve and accentuate her long shapely legs.

An envelope in the bottom of the box caught his eye. He couldn't resist picking it up. Feeling guilty, but not guilty enough to stop snooping, he slid the card from the envelope and silently read it.

Now that you've had
A birthday, you're
Old enough to wear
This.

I dare you.

Love, Me

Scowling, Dakota crammed the card back in the envelope, returned it and the red teddy to the gift box, then stalked from the room. Pokey trailed after him.

After he'd changed his clothes, Dakota went down to the tennis court and slammed balls back at the automatic feeder.

An hour later he was in the shower when Pokey, who was waiting outside the door, began to bark. The moment Dakota turned off the water he could hear the cause of Pokey's excitement: a commotion outside in the driveway with cars honking like a procession of newlyweds just leaving the church.

Pokey only added to the din with her yelping as she ran back and forth between him and the door, begging him to come.

"Let me put my pants on, okay?" Dakota said, when Pokey came over and swatted at him with her paw to get him to hurry.

Pokey settled down, but the honking didn't.

Finally decent, he ran his hands through his wet hair to comb it, and started downstairs. In his hurry he hadn't bothered with shoes, which was a mistake; at the bottom of the stairs he stepped on a thorn Pokey must have carried in on her fur.

Swearing, he pulled the thorn from his foot, then hopped to the front door and opened it to see what in hell was the cause of all the racket.

It was not a parade, it was only one car. Chelsea sat in the front seat pressing the horn, looking as pleased as a blue ribbon winner.

Tucker was sprawled in the back seat with his leg propped up.

It wasn't just any car.

The reason for the smug look plastered on Chelsea's face was the fact that it was *his* car—an exact replica of the car she'd totaled.

8

FOR SEVERAL SECONDS Dakota simply stared in amazement. "I don't believe this," he said finally, as he began limping carefully across the driveway. "Where did you get it?"

Chelsea grinned and lovingly patted the decrepit hunk of metal. "Tucker tracked it down. He was on your phone for hours until he found one."

"Long distance," Tucker called from the back seat.

When Dakota looked his way, Tucker tipped his baseball cap. "Don't know if it's going to work for you, dude. I rode here in the back seat all the way, and I haven't had any tunes pop into my head. Course, I mighta been a little more inspired if I'd had a woman back here to keep me company."

"Have you *ever* had any tunes pop into your head, Tucker?" Chelsea demanded. She was distracted by Dakota's half-naked body; he was like a golden cougar, all ripply sinew and sleek lines. And he looked like he'd just crawled out of bed. Had they interrupted something? She blushed, hoping

Melinda Jackson wasn't going to come sashaying out of the house at any moment.

"Nope, can't say as I have," Tucker answered with a wide grin. "I'm a lover, not a writer."

"Well, what do you think?" Chelsea turned to ask Dakota, trying not to stare at where his jeans were riding low on his hips.

"I think it's—" he ran his hand through his hair, "—it's something, all right."

"But do you think it will work? Do you think you'll be able to write again now?"

Dakota smoothed his hand over the fender, feeling the dents, a thoughtful look on his face. "I'm willing to give it a try, since the two of you have gone to all this effort." He shrugged. "Who knows? I suppose stranger things have happened."

"Well, then, someone had better help me haul my butt outta here." Tucker groaned, trying to maneuver from the back seat.

Dakota went to give him a hand.

"Thanks for helping locate the car," Dakota said when he'd pulled Tucker out.

"No thanks needed. I'd do anything at all to get Chelsea the song she wants. And even if I hadn't wanted to help, she'd have made me. You may have noticed the woman does get her way."

"I've noticed."

"You'd better get inside and off that leg," Chelsea ordered, lifting his arm across her shoulders to help him hobble inside.

Dakota walked on ahead to get the door.

"You're looking a little gimpy there yourself, dude," Tucker observed.

"I stepped on a thorn."

"Did you put something on it?" Chelsea asked, as Dakota helped her lower Tucker to the sofa in the library.

"No, it's nothing."

"You sit down there with Tucker, and I'll get some antiseptic."

"I'd sit if I were you," Tucker said with a laugh. "That is, after you get me a cola, if you've got one. We didn't stop to eat."

"I'll get us something to drink and see what the cook left for dinner," Dakota offered.

Chelsea returned with a tube of ointment just as Dakota came back, carrying a tray. He put the tray on the coffee table and handed out drinks, then set out soup bowls for each of them.

"What is this?" Tucker asked, peering suspiciously into the mixture Dakota ladled into the bowl in front of him.

"Gazpacho."

"Bless you." Tucker dipped his spoon into it, sipped and made a terrible face. "Tastes like cold tomato soup to me. Think I'll order a pizza instead. Anyone else want some?"

"Tucker, you're such a provincial."

"I don't think that was a compliment, do you, Dakota?" Tucker reached for the phone. "I'm ordering the works, any takers?"

Chelsea and Dakota shook their heads no.

But when the pizza came, Chelsea and Dakota hijacked it, and sat across the room eating it and laughing at Tucker's threats, which got more inventive as the pizza disappeared.

When there were only three pieces left, they took pity on Tucker and handed over the remaining pizza.

"Just for that I'm not going to let you guys sing at my concert," Tucker said around a bite of pizza.

"What concert? I thought the tour ended in St. Louis," Chelsea said.

"It did. I've decided to get together a special concert to aid the flood victims. I was lucky. All I lost was a tour bus. Thousands of people lost everything they owned in the flood. I think I owe a debt of gratitude for my life being spared."

"What a great idea, Tucker!" Chelsea exclaimed. "I don't know about Dakota, but I'm singing. Maybe if the car idea works, I can sing the new song Dakota's going to write for me."

"Count me in, too," Dakota said, as Chelsea reached for the antiseptic. She lifted his bare foot onto her lap and began applying the ointment to the thorn wound.

"Ouch! That burns like hell," he complained, jerking his foot away.

"Don't be such a baby. Now it will heal properly. It wouldn't do a thing for my image, you know, to have two men on crutches flanking me onstage."

"We need to set a date for the concert, and it should be soon. Everyone's needs are immediate. Think we can pull it together in two weeks?" Tucker asked, looking at the two of them.

"We?" Chelsea and Dakota chorused.

"Don't get all excited. I'm going to be the boss, but I'll need a couple of people to help get it together in time."

"Okay, I'll volunteer to take care of publicity," Chelsea offered.

"You always do," Tucker mumbled.

"What was that?"

"I said you're good at getting publicity—just make sure this publicity is good."

"And I'll help line up the country singers," Dakota volunteered.

"Okay, good. Then all I need to do is line up the rest of the talent. It'll give me something to do to keep me from going nuts while I'm immobilized."

"We need to make a list of possibilities," Chelsea suggested.

"I'll get pens and paper." Dakota pulled out the desk drawers until he'd located two pens and some paper.

He handed a pen and a couple of sheets of paper to Chelsea, but kept the rest for himself. "I'm going outside and try out the car," he announced.

IT DIDN'T WORK.

It didn't matter how long Dakota sat in the back seat, he was still blocked.

It didn't even help when Chelsea joined him.

Nothing worked.

Chelsea wasn't surprised. She suspected that the real reason for Dakota's writer's block had to do with the way he kept his emotions under lock and key.

Dakota had left his past behind, but he couldn't seem to escape its effect.

Chelsea admired him for giving up his family, money and connections for what he loved to do.

He'd willingly given up what she'd never had and longed for.

It was clear to her that Dakota needed to let go emotionally to be able to write.

And it was all up to her.

Which was just how she liked it. She believed in herself, and trusted no one. Her family background had left its own imprint.

She could love and nurture Tucker because she was sure of his feelings for her.

To get Dakota to open himself to how he felt, she was going to have to persuade him to let himself be vulnerable—vulnerable enough to express his emotions to another.

It wasn't going to be an easy task, for she knew loving someone was a scary proposition. She knew how badly it hurt when you gave someone the power not to love you back.

"THIS LOOKS LIKE FUN," Chelsea said, as she studied an ad in the newspaper the following morning.

"What?" Tucker looked up from the latest name he'd added to the growing list of performers who'd agreed to do the Flood-Aid concert.

"A psychic fair. It says there are going to be fortune-tellers, palm readers, tarot cards.... Come on, why don't we all go?" Chelsea said, looking from Tucker to Dakota.

"Palm readers?" Dakota echoed skeptically.

"Oh, come on, don't be such a stuffed shirt. Maybe one can tell us when you're going to get over your writer's block. I'm not leaving till you do, you know."

"I'd go if I were you. Otherwise you'll be having nightmares about having us for permanent house-guests," Tucker warned.

"What about you, aren't you coming, Tucker?"

"No, I'm not very good on crutches, yet. Pokey and I will stay here and try to talk the cook into making something we've heard of for dinner."

Chelsea rolled her eyes at Dakota. "Hope you like macaroni and cheese with Twinkies snacks for dessert."

"Maybe we'll eat dinner out," Dakota said, getting up. "Don't wait for us."

"Then you're going?" Chelsea asked, surprised he was agreeing to her plan so easily.

"I've learned arguing with you is a waste of energy. Besides, I really would like to know if you two are going to be permanent houseguests."

"Whatever happened to Southern hospitality?" Chelsea teased.

"We save it for invited guests."

The psychic fair was held in a park near the center of Nashville. A large crowd milled about the colorful tents and the sweet scent of apple fritters drifted on the breeze.

"Are you sure about this?" Dakota asked a bit nervously as they slipped on dark sunglasses in an effort to disguise their faces.

"Oh, for heaven's sake, Dakota, lighten up. They aren't going to put a curse on you."

"No, *you* already did that."

"Well, then, maybe we can find someone who knows how to break the evil spell I've put on you, okay? Now which one do you want to try first?"

"First?"

"Sure, we'll keep going until we get a fortune we can live with."

"You're a piece of work, Chelsea Stone," he said, shaking his head.

"I think that one over there looks pretty interesting." She tugged on his arm and they made their way through the crowd until they reached the tent where a woman sat with a Paisley shawl draped over her table.

"How much?" Chelsea asked the woman who studied them with shrewd dark eyes.

"For both of you?"

"No, just him. I know my future."

"Twenty-five dollars," the woman quoted.

Dakota reached for his wallet, but Chelsea stopped him. "My treat."

The woman motioned for the two of them to be seated in the folding chairs set in front of the table.

"Past, present or future?" she asked, looking at Dakota as she warmed the crystal ball before her with her beringed hands.

"Whatever," Dakota replied with a shrug, not bothering to hide the fact that he wasn't a believer in the supernatural.

The fortune-teller waited for him to choose anyway.

"Past," he said finally.

"There's no future in the past," Chelsea objected. "Tell us the present."

The woman looked at Dakota, and he nodded.

She peered into the crystal ball, waiting for the cloudiness to clear and present her with a picture she could read. Finally she was ready. "Yes, I see it. There is a young woman. She will cling to you. It will be very difficult for you to get away from her."

"Tell me about it," he muttered, laughing at the look on Chelsea's face. "Can you give me some sort of potion to get rid of her?"

"It won't be necessary. She will leave you for the man who is right for her."

Dakota frowned.

"What about his future?" Chelsea quickly asked.

The woman looked at the ball intently. "Yes, yes, it is very good."

"It is?" Dakota sounded surprised.

"I see many, many women falling in love with you."

"You know this fortune-telling stuff ain't so bad," he said, turning to smile at Chelsea.

"Ah, but I see there is only one woman who loves you," the woman added.

"What about his career? What do you see in store for his career?"

The woman shook her head. "It is not going to go on.... I see it stopping," she said to Dakota, who swore.

"No, wait...." The woman wasn't finished with her prediction.

"Your career is going to change. And when it does, I see a great fortune."

"I've heard enough," Dakota said, getting up. "I have no intention of going back home to join the family banking business."

"There is one more thing—" the woman began, but Dakota cut her off.

"I don't want to know," he said, and waited impatiently while Chelsea paid the fee.

"Why would you not want to know that today is your lucky day?" the woman asked Dakota as she handed Chelsea her change.

"What do you want to do now?" Chelsea asked as Dakota led her away from the tent.

"Anything but have my fortune told, thank you," he grumbled.

"Oh, let's get an apple fritter," she said, as they approached the line waiting for the hot delicacy.

"Okay, you wait in line here. I'll get us something to drink over there," he agreed. Chelsea watched him head for the other line and wondered about the wisdom of coming to the psychic fair.

She believed in fortune-tellers just enough to be concerned about what the woman had said about Dakota's career ending.

She finally reached the front of the line and purchased two apple fritters, then turned to look for Dakota. He wasn't in the drink line any longer, and she didn't see him at first. Then she spotted him.

The fortune-teller's prediction was already coming true: A golden-haired toddler had fastened her arms around Dakota's leg.

Chelsea laughed out loud at Dakota's predicament.

"It's not funny," he said, when she joined him.

"Who is she?"

"I don't know. I can't get her to talk to me. And she is holding on for dear life. I keep waiting for the police to come and arrest me," he said nervously.

Chelsea went down on one knee to talk to the little girl.

"Hi, what's your name, sugar?"

Blue eyes round as saucers stared at Chelsea, but the child wouldn't say a word.

"Would you like a bite?" Chelsea asked, offering her the apple fritter in her hand.

The toddler turned her face away.

"Where did she come from?" Chelsea asked, looking up at Dakota.

"I don't know. I was in line and next thing I knew, I felt someone hanging on to my leg."

"Well, she has to belong to someone. . . ." She tapped the little girl on her shoulder. "Where's your mommy, sugar? Is she lost?"

The child turned back to stare at her, but said nothing.

Chelsea set her plate of apple fritter down and tried to lift the little girl, but she wouldn't let go of Dakota's leg. "Well, looks like the fortune-teller was right. It's going to be very difficult for you to get away from her." Chelsea laughed.

"It's not funny," Dakota repeated.

"Oh, come on, Dakota. Relax. The fortune-teller said she'll leave you for the man who's right for her," Chelsea teased.

"So why do I have the feeling that will be when I'm giving her away at her wedding?" he asked, taking a gulp of soda.

"Emily . . . Em-ily . . . Where are you . . . ?"

They spotted the long-legged man in jeans at the same time. "Over here!" Chelsea called out, signaling to the man. "I think we have her."

The man strode toward them and a smile lit up his face when he saw the toddler. "Emily, baby, what are you doing?"

The little girl let go of Dakota's leg and reached up her hands, saying, "Da-da . . . Da."

Her father laughed. "We were talking to friends and I let go of her. I guess she thought she had *my* leg."

"Well, she's safe and that's all that matters," Chelsea said. She waved as the pixie and her father moved off to find the child's mother.

"So, you want to try another psychic?" Chelsea asked, breaking off a piece of apple fritter and feeding it to Dakota.

"Why not? It's my lucky day, right?"

"I'll let you pick this time," Chelsea said, ignoring his sarcasm.

"How about none of the above," he said, leaning forward to brush a speck of powdered sugar from her nose.

"One more?" she coaxed.

"Tucker's right about you, you know that? All right, one more."

They tossed their trash in a metal drum and headed back to the grouping of tents.

"Let's try a palm reader this time," she suggested.

They strolled over to a tent hung with a banner advertising Madame Marie. Inside the tent was a young woman reading a textbook.

"Can I help you?" she asked, looking up from the book.

"He wants his palm read."

"I don't want my palm read, I'm having my palm read," Dakota whispered as he sat down.

"Let me see both hands, please," Madame Marie said.

Dakota put them on the table and the young woman ran her fingers over them, nodding and observing.

"Is there anything special you'd like to know?" she asked, before she began.

"Yeah, what course are you taking?" he asked, indicating the textbook.

"Journalism," she answered good-naturedly. "I want to be a writer."

"So do I," Dakota muttered under his breath.

The young woman was busy studying his hands and didn't hear him, but Chelsea glared at him.

"You're artistic," she said, not looking up for confirmation. "You have a strong lifeline." She paused then, studying his palm. "Your career—now it looks like there's a . . ."

"Problem?" Dakota filled in the word, resigned.

"A change. There's a fork in your career path, but it runs very close and parallel. . . . That's odd. I've not seen that before."

"What does it mean?" Chelsea asked.

"I'd say that whatever the career change, it won't be far afield from what he's doing now."

"And it's my lucky day, right?" Dakota said sardonically.

"I don't know, is it?"

"Not so far."

"It's early," Chelsea said defensively.

"How about you? Would you like your palm read?" the woman asked.

"No. No, thanks. I'm supersensitive."

After Dakota had paid the woman and they'd left the tent, he asked. "Supersensitive?"

"Well, I am."

"What does that make me, a clod?"

"No, not sensitive like that. I meant I'm suggestible. If someone tells me I'm going to win the lottery, fall in love, and get a hangnail, all I remember is I'm going to get a hangnail. So I don't like to let anyone suggest bad things to me."

"But I'm fair game."

"You're a tough guy," she said evasively.

"Yeah, a tough guy with no future, if you've been paying attention."

"Oh, Dakota, you don't really believe all this stuff, do you?"

"Wait a minute, if you don't believe in it, then why did you drag me here?"

"For fun. Fun, Dakota. It's an interesting concept. Haven't you heard of it?" This wasn't working at all, she thought, miserable that she was failing in her plan to draw Dakota out. She was only making him feel worse.

"I think you have fun and torture confused," he said, confirming her worst suspicions. "And believe me, I know what torture is. Torture is when you drag an artist with writer's block to a psychic who tells him his career is over. Torture is when you wear jean shorts with holes in scandalous places and a white eyelet bra and call it an outfit. Torture is . . ."

That did it. She tugged his arm. "You want fun, flat-out fun, then come with me."

"What? Where are we going?" he demanded as she led him from the park to the car.

"Don't worry, it's your lucky day, remember?"

Ten minutes later she directed him to pull into the parking lot of a convenience store.

"Give me all your money," she said, turning to him.

"Aren't you supposed to put the stocking cap on first and then go inside the store before you say that?"

"Cute. Come on, empty your wallet."

"You're serious."

"No, I'm having fun," she said, holding out her hand for the money. "Come on, let the moths out, open your wallet and give me all your bills. No holding out, either. I want every single one."

"Are you practicing for divorce court?"

"Quit stalling, tough guy, and hand it over."

He opened his wallet, withdrew all the bills and handed them over.

She arranged them in numerical order, and counted up sixty-two dollars.

"Be back in a flash," she said with a wicked wink. "Don't get any bright ideas about leaving."

"Why? Am I driving the getaway car? Is trouble your idea of fun?" he asked, as she slammed the door.

She leaned in the window, well aware of the generous view she flashed him. "Haven't you read the tabloids? I'm trouble on the hoof. Y'all just sit tight and I'll be right back with a sackful of fun."

"What in the world?" he demanded when she returned with a paper bag filled with scratch-off lottery tickets, pulled them out, divided them and handed him a coin.

"It's your lucky day, remember?"

"What are you going to do with the money we win, assuming we win any?"

"I'm sure you'll want to donate it to the Flood-Aid concert."

Sixty-two tickets, plus seven free tickets later, they had scratched off a total of five hundred and two dollars.

"You're right, that was fun," Dakota agreed, handing over the money for her to give to Tucker. "Now what?"

"Now let's have some wild fun."

"I shudder to ask. . . ."

"I thought we'd go rollerblading."

"Yeah, right. I'm going rollerblading with a charm-school dropout. I've already got a wounded foot that feels like you poured a gallon of peroxide on it."

"Shut up and drive, tough guy. I'm going to make you have fun if it kills you."

And it nearly did.

"Remind me to take you snipe hunting when I can walk again," he grumbled a couple of hours later, as he limped ahead of her into the house.

"What's snipe hunting?" she asked. She took a tray of ice out of the refrigerator to make an ice pack for the lump on his forehead.

"It's a quaint regional custom," he answered, groaning when she applied the makeshift ice pack to the bump on his head.

"You wouldn't have gotten all banged up if you'd worn kneepads, wrist guards and a helmet like me. They have all the rollerblading gear for a reason."

"Yes, to make you look ridiculous. Do you realize I felt like Mad Max?"

"Oh, right, and you didn't look ridiculous when you pirouetted over that Dalmatian and landed headfirst in the trash receptacle with your rollerblade wheels still spinning?"

Chelsea shook her head as she looked at him. Okay, so maybe he didn't *feel* vulnerable—she hadn't succeeded in getting him to let go completely—but he *looked* vulnerable. Wasn't that half the battle?

9

CHELSEA TURNED OFF the shower with a flick of her wrist, then grabbed the thick terry towel as she stepped from the shower stall into the steamy bathroom. Leisurely dabbing the moisture from her body, she let her mind wander over the day she'd spent with Dakota.

The first image to flash into her mind was that of the little girl who'd clung to Dakota's leg. Dakota had truly looked panicked. The toddler had scared him because he hadn't known how to relate to her.

Just as he didn't know how to relate to her. Chelsea knew that she scared him because she was constantly challenging him. She wouldn't let him withdraw and run from his feelings, feelings she knew he was going to have to explore in order to be able to write the song for her.

She understood Dakota, she really did. He mirrored her own fear of failure. They both feared losing because their careers were all either of them really had.

She tossed aside the damp towel, pulled on a pair of white cotton panties and slipped into a short, silky navy-and-white print dress. She put her hair up in a loose French twist and smiled at her reflection in the mirror as she recalled how awkward Dakota had looked at first on the rollerblades. Unfortunately, just as he'd become confident enough to try turning on them, the Dalmatian had darted into his path.

Chelsea felt she'd made progress in her efforts to draw Dakota out emotionally, but she was afraid if she didn't act quickly he'd retreat again behind his wall of well-mannered aloofness.

Reaching for a hairpin, she accidentally knocked her bottle of red nail polish to the floor. As she bent to retrieve it, she got an idea about what to do next in her campaign to loosen up Dakota.

"DAMN!" DAKOTA ROLLED up yet another piece of paper and tossed it aside. He'd been sitting in bed trying to write a song since he'd showered, but his aches and scrapes from rollerblading kept distracting him.

No, that wasn't true. They were a minor distraction compared to Chelsea Stone. She was making him nuts. He couldn't even put her out of his mind for the length of time it took to write a song. While he was trying to write about the romance of an imaginary woman, she loitered in his mind, wearing not much of anything as she always did.

It amazed him that Tucker allowed her to dress the way she did. Didn't she realize the effect she had—or was that why she did it?

It was odd. Her sexy way of dressing wasn't really seductive. It was more a dare, more a statement of the fact that she was in charge; that she would wear what she wanted and didn't care who didn't like it.

The problem was he liked it. He liked it all too much.

And it made him crazy because he didn't approve of her. Didn't approve of her teasing him when she was involved with Tucker.

He rolled up another piece of paper he'd scribbled on and tossed it on the floor in frustration.

Concentrate. He had to concentrate. One song would get her out of his life.

The only article of clothing he had on was a pair of old jeans. He'd thought they'd be comfortable, but the soft material rubbed the scrape on his knee and it throbbed, distracting him.

He tapped his pen on the pad of paper on his lap, jotted down words, then crossed them out. Frustrated, he plumped the pillows bracing him against the brass headboard, and rested his feet on Pokey.

He ripped the sheet of paper from the pad and began again. It looked as if it had snowed balls of crumpled paper around him. They were littered everywhere—on the bed and all over the hardwood floor.

A knock sounded on the bedroom door.

Pokey's ears pricked up.

"Go away," Dakota called out.

Pokey whined an invitation.

Chelsea ignored Dakota's inhospitality and entered the room.

"You're writing!"

"No, I'm not," Dakota said. His tone was surly.

"But of course, you are. What's all this paper, if you're not?" she asked, picking up a crumpled ball. "Are you and Pokey having a paper-ball fight?"

"No, I'm *trying* to write. If I were actually writing, there wouldn't be any crumpled paper, just a nice stack of songs in various stages of completion."

"But at least you're trying. . . ."

"That's all I've been doing for the past six months."

Chelsea reached to scratch Pokey behind the ears, then picked up one of the crumpled balls of paper lying on the floor beside her. She began uncrumpling it, but before she could finish the task, Dakota lunged to grab it from her.

"Was there something you wanted?" he asked, tossing the paper ball across the room.

She shook the bottle of red nail polish in her hand. "I want you to paint my toenails for me."

"What?"

"You know, put polish on my toenails. Don't tell me you've never painted a woman's toenails before."

"Does Tucker do that for you?"

"Sometimes."

"So why don't you get him to do it for you now?"

"Because he's not here. He left a note that he was going out with a couple of members of his band who're going to help with the Flood-Aid concert."

"Well, I'm not going to polish your toenails, you can forget that." He could almost feel himself blushing.

"I'll do something for you. What would you like me to do for you, Dakota?" she asked. She sat down on the bed.

She had to be blind if she didn't see what he really wanted her to do for him. Instead he said, "Leaving would be good. Forget that you want me to write you a song."

"How about a foot massage?" she suggested. "Maybe it will make you forget getting banged up when you fell."

"How is massaging my feet going to help that?" he demanded. She sat cross-legged on the bed and hauled his foot into her lap.

"There are nerves below the surface of the skin that are sensitive to touch. When you stimulate them they block pain in other parts of the body," she explained, rubbing and applying pressure to the sole of his foot.

"Did you work in a massage parlor? Is that how you know all that?"

"No, Tucker taught me."

Dakota groaned.

He closed his eyes and let her fingers work their magic.

"Relax," she said as she worked her fingers around his ankle. "I swear you'd think no one had ever given you a foot massage before."

He didn't think anyone had. And certainly not holding his foot in their lap while wearing a short silky dress that allowed the occasional glimpse of white panties. Lord, there was no way he was going to be able to hold her foot in his lap to paint her toenails.

"Here, give me your other foot," she said, when she was finished with the first one. He wondered if she knew what the hell she was doing. Probably. She had one thing right—he wasn't feeling any pain.

Except in one place.

Her touch was velvety soft.

And he was rock hard.

She'd been right. The scrape on his knee was no longer throbbing. The throbbing had switched to another part of his body.

"That's enough," he said, struggling for some semblance of his sanity.

"Okay, your turn," she said, tossing him the nail polish.

He had to do something quickly before she decided to plop her foot into his lap and discovered the effect she was having on him. He reached behind him, grabbed a pillow and tossed it at her. "Here, let's trade places," he said, levering himself from the mound of pillows.

For once she didn't give him any argument, and they switched places.

He braced himself on one elbow and opened the bottle of red polish.

Pokey got a whiff of it and leaped off the bed. "You're right, this stuff does stink, Pokey," Dakota said, making a face. He made a little dent in the comforter and nestled the open bottle so it wouldn't spill, then pulled Chelsea's foot to rest against his chest.

Chelsea laughed as he began painting her toenails.

"What's so funny?" he asked, intent on what he was doing.

"You're concentrating so hard your brow is breaking out in a sweat."

"I am not—" He glanced up and then quickly looked away from the sleek expanse of her sunkissed legs and the juncture where her dress pooled.

"Damn!" he swore, looking back down at what he was doing.

She sat up and demanded, "What's wrong?"

"I painted the edge of your baby toe." He wiped at the wet polish with his finger, but only made it worse.

She leaned back against the pillows, unconcerned. "Don't worry about it. I'll get it off later with some polish remover."

He set her foot back down on the bed, and motioned for her to give him her other one.

She slid her foot toward him as he dabbed the brush back into the bottle of polish.

"Oopsies . . ." she said, lifting her polished toes beneath his nose. "You forgot to blow on my toes."

"What?"

"You need to blow on my toes so they'll dry quicker," she explained with a playful grin.

He grudgingly complied, and she giggled.

"What's so funny?" he demanded.

"Your breath is hot."

Dakota had the look of a man going before a firing squad, but he gamely took her other foot and began dabbing the red polish on her toenails.

"I was thinking we could go out to dinner," Chelsea said boldly. "I feel like dressing up."

"I'd rather not." He lifted her foot to blow on the polish.

"Well, that's blunt enough." Chelsea pulled her foot from his grasp and started to get off the bed.

"I'd rather not go out. . . ."

"I got it. You'd rather not go out to dinner with me. Fine. I'm a big girl. I can have dinner alone. Don't worry about it," she said, standing.

"No, you don't understand. I meant I'd rather not go *out* to dinner," he explained. "The cook made my favorite meal and I've been looking forward to it. I thought we could eat in, but you can dress up if you'd like."

"I think I will," she said, brightening. "What time is dinner?"

"As soon as you can get dressed. The meal is keeping warm in the oven for us. Come on downstairs when you're dressed." He screwed the cap back on the nail polish and tossed the bottle to her. "After all, it'd be a shame not to get dressed up with your toes all ready to party."

"You have to dress for dinner, too," she said, eyeing his ragged jeans.

"Of course."

After she left, Dakota went to his closet. He stood looking through it, trying to decide what would dress up his jeans.

CHELSEA SMOOTHED THE body-hugging red dress she wore one more time before going downstairs to join Dakota for dinner. She didn't know why, but she was nervous. Maybe it was because a half hour ago he'd been blowing on her toes. The sexual chemistry between them still hummed, as unresolved as the issue of his writing a song for her.

The first thing she saw when she entered the warm, country-style kitchen was Dakota's jeans-encased tush and bare back as he bent to reach into the oven.

"I thought you were going to dress for dinner," she said as she came up behind him.

He withdrew a sheet of flaky biscuits and set it down on the tile counter, next to a covered casserole in a basket holder. He turned and flipped the tie around his neck. "I did dress for dinner."

She shook her head. "Wrong. No Shoes, No Shirt, No Service. Didn't you read the sign?"

"What sign?"

"Go and dress for dinner. I'll take care of setting the table."

Dakota rolled his eyes. "Yes, ma'am. When you're wearing a dress like that, I'll do anything you ask me to."

Ten minutes later she had the small bistro table in the kitchen covered with linen and set with silver, and had put a candle in the center of the table. She found some chamber music on the radio and was just lighting the candle when Dakota returned.

"So, what do you think?" he asked, bowing.

She turned, her eyes raking the elegant tuxedo he'd donned. "I think you look like a maître d'."

"In that case, *madame*," he said, and with a flourish pulled back her chair and shook out her napkin.

Chelsea sat and allowed him to bring the food to the table. "I guess tuxedos weren't that unusual at your dinner table at home, were they?" she asked, when he sat down.

"Let's just say, jeans and a tie wouldn't have cut it with my mother."

After ladling out a bowl of stew for each of them, Chelsea tried again. "I'm sure you know everyone has read about your family background and is aware they don't approve of your becoming a country singer. But don't you think that now you've become such a big success, they'd accept you?"

"Then what would I have?" he asked, flippantly.

"A family..." Chelsea's voice held an undisguised note of longing.

"A family? You've got to be joking. That's not what my idea of a family is. To me a family accepts you for who you are, not what you have or what you do."

"Are you sure you're not being a little hard on your family?"

"Oh yeah, I'm sure. You see, the reason my family's blood is so blue is because it's icy cold. That's why country music appeals to me. It's music about feelings. Real emotion. That's something my family is clueless about. They were only concerned about appearances. How they appeared was much more important than what they actually were."

"You sound pretty bitter."

"No, I just resent what they did to me."

"You can undo it, you know. You don't have to live the rest of your life closed off from your feelings as they were."

"I'm not closed off from my feelings," he retorted, taking an angry bite of the biscuit he'd buttered.

"Then why don't I have a song from you?"

"What about *your* family?" he asked, avoiding her question.

"What about them?"

"Are you close to them?"

"No." Her answer was short and final, and did not invite follow-up questions.

Dakota ignored the door she'd closed. "Why not?"

"I'm just not."

"Look who's talking about being closed off from their feelings...."

Chelsea laid down her fork, and looked at him consideringly. Finally she made up her mind to discuss with him something she'd never discussed with anyone but Tucker.

"I ran away from home when I was a teenager."

"That's a pretty dangerous thing to do, especially for a girl."

"You're right, it is. But it wasn't something impetuous. My parents were abusive. I knew there was a very real chance I could end up dead, so the risk of running away was relative. I took care of myself by leaving."

"Didn't your parents try to find you?"

"For that they would have had to sober up," she said, getting up to clear the plates. Dakota sensed that it was painful for her to talk about her parents so he dropped the subject.

"So how good is this pecan pie?" Chelsea asked as she brought it to the table.

"Sinfully good," Dakota assured her. He served them each a slice.

"Mind if we change that funeral music?" he asked. "It reminds me too much of dinners at home. Let's see if I can't find something a little more uptempo." He got up and played with the radio until he found a decent pop station.

"Rock and roll, Dakota? Isn't that heresy in this house?"

He made a mock bow and returned to his seat. "It's in your honor—Southern hospitality, you know. So, what do you think of the pecan pie?"

Chelsea took another bite of the still-warm pie. "Mmm . . . you were right. It is sinfully good. I can taste the rich, dark syrup."

"I don't know about that. All I know is that I like it."

"Close your eyes," Chelsea instructed.

"Why?"

"Just close them."

He complied. "Now what?"

"Tell me what your senses tell you."

"I smell food."

"What kind of food?"

"I don't know. Food." He opened his eyes. "What did you expect me to say?"

She closed her eyes.

"I smell the wine in the stew gravy, the sweet fragrance of the geraniums blooming on the windowsill, the acrid burning of the candle wick, and the spicy scent of your cologne. I hear the radio playing a golden oldie, the whisper of the ceiling fan overhead, and your breathing. I feel the breeze from the ceiling fan and the light scratch of lace across my breasts."

She opened her eyes to see Dakota's gaze on her cleavage. He looked up into her eyes.

"You can't write the kind of song I want, Dakota, if you don't allow yourself to really feel. When I sing, I sing from my heart. I can't sing a song that isn't written for me from the heart."

On the radio Rod Stewart's raspy voice began one of his sexy ballads.

"Dance with me," Dakota said, rising from his chair. "Let me show you how I feel."

Chelsea melted into his arms. In her high-heeled sandals, she fitted against him perfectly.

Dakota was a good slow-dancer, his lead authoritative, his hold on her loose, yet possessive. As they swirled around the kitchen she drank in his seductive scent and reveled in the feel of his lean, hard body brushing hers.

He pulled her in closer and purposely slowed their steps until they were rocking gently together. She quivered as his lips caressed her earlobe, then kissed the spot where the curve of her neck met her shoulder.

There was no question that the dance was foreplay.

No question where the evening was leading.

No question how Dakota felt.

Until he bent her back into a low dip when the song ended. A dip that flashed the red teddy she wore under the body-hugging dress.

When he brought Chelsea out of the dip, she could see that his mood had changed. He released her abruptly and stepped back from her.

"What's wrong?" One minute she'd felt the heat of his full-out sensual assault; the next, she felt the iciness of his anger.

"There are a few things about you that are common knowledge, too, and the truth is I don't see myself writing a song for a woman with a tattoo no-telling-where on her body."

Chelsea went very quiet. So that was it. He'd come to his senses, remembering she wasn't good enough for him.

Her dark eyes flashed a white-hot fury. "It's not hard to tell where, Dakota. I'll show you."

With that, she kicked off her heels, one of which bounced off his shin.

"Ouch!"

Ignoring his complaint, she peeled off her red dress and tossed it at him.

He caught it with one hand.

"What are you doing?"

She slid the straps of the red teddy from her shoulders, pushed it down and stepped out of it. She kicked it aside and walked toward him, completely naked.

"What are you doing?" he demanded, his eyes wide, drinking in her beauty.

"I'm satisfying your curiosity. You were speculating about where the tattoo is on my body. Now you don't have to speculate. She turned her leg so he could see the tiny rose and delicate script on the inside of her ankle.

"What does it say?"

"It's Tucker's nickname."

"How charming." His tone was condescending, a deliberate put-down. "And I suppose it's true that he has your name tattooed on his body."

"That's right." She did her best not to let the bright smile she flashed him quiver.

"How about you, Dakota?"

"What about me?"

"Aren't you going to show me your tattoo?"

"I don't have one."

"You mean like you don't have a heart?"

"That's right," he retorted. "But at least I don't get my kicks playing one lover off against another."

"What's that supposed to mean?" Chelsea demanded, still too angry to be embarrassed that she was standing naked in Dakota's kitchen.

"It means you trying to seduce me while you and Tucker are lovers. Does it give you some kind of kick to wear his gift while doing it?"

"What are you talking about?"

Dakota nodded at the teddy on the floor.

So that was it. He'd seen the card. Dakota had been snooping in her room. And then he had the nerve to challenge her with his holier-than-thou attitude. She found herself wanting to strike out at him, wanting to hurt him as he'd hurt her.

"What's the matter, Dakota, you afraid you won't measure up to Tucker?"

That got to him. He gave up any pretense of control. He reached out, shoved his hand into her long curls and drew her to him, then lowered his lips to hers in a punishing kiss.

His mouth took total possession of hers, staking a claim that meant to erase any other. The hunger of his kiss was urgent, demanding her response.

She felt herself responding shamelessly, even knowing his kiss was one of anger and sexual jealousy. His kiss revealed a man capable of strong feelings.

"This isn't a good idea," Chelsea said, her voice shaky, when he broke off the deep kiss.

"I think it is. We've both wanted this from the beginning. You know we have. Say it," he coaxed, his breath warm on her ear.

"I want you," she said as his lips moved down her throat, exploring.

"Come here, sweetheart," he urged. He backed up until they reached the table, then he dropped down into the chair. Chelsea stood before him, held by his gaze.

"You're beautiful, sweetheart, you know that." He used both hands to explore her body. His fingertips seared her skin wherever they roamed. She moved closer against his hands when they closed over her rounded breasts, then kneaded them gently.

She jerked involuntarily and sighed as his fingers tweaked their peaks. Moving ever lower, his hands measured her small waist and slid over her hips to cup her buttocks.

A slight gasp escaped her lips when he moved one hand back around to the front of her body to slip it between her thighs. He nudged her legs apart while the hand remaining on her buttocks pressed her to move against the hand that cupped her sex.

She found herself unable to resist his coaxing, felt herself irresistibly responding as waves of hot desire flooded her.

Whimpering when he thrust two fingers into her dewy mound, she began following his lead and moved against his insistent hand.

"That's it, sweetheart. Rock for me. Rock and roll. Let me see your pleasure. A little faster... now slower... Come on, sweetheart, you're almost there. Yes... that's it, sweetheart."

Mewing and breathless, she came apart for him.

10

DAKOTA PULLED CHELSEA down into his lap, where he stroked her face and murmured sweet love words as she lay deliciously limp in his arms.

Her eyes fluttered closed and she reveled in his touch.

"Don't go to sleep on me now, sweetheart," he said, loosening his tuxedo tie. "Give me a hand undressing here, would you? I'm feeling just a tad overdressed."

Chelsea stirred. "We need to talk," she mumbled, but she helped him push his jacket off his shoulders, then tugged it down his arms until he was free of it.

"Later. We'll talk later."

His kiss silenced her objection. He didn't have to urge her to continue helping him undress; she took the initiative. Her hands reached to unbuckle the black cummerbund at his narrow waist. When the cummerbund dropped to the floor, she undid the tricky cuff links, then helped him shimmy out of his shirt.

She unbuttoned his pants, but his hands stopped her from going further. "I think I'd better handle this," he said. He set her gently on her feet, then stood to undertake the precarious task of unzipping his very strained fly.

"No, I want to handle it," Chelsea teased, pressing her hand against his fly and making the task even more difficult.

"Cut it out, woman," he said with a stern look and ignored her giggles as he managed to undo the zipper without damage to his body. His pants fell to his ankles and he went to step out of them, but tripped when they caught at the shoes he'd forgotten to remove in his haste to shed his clothes.

He landed with a thud and a curse on the glossy wood floor of the kitchen. He sat up, yanked off one shoe, then the other, and tossed them at Chelsea who wasn't even trying to hide her amusement.

He finally kicked free of his trousers, and was reaching to shed his socks when Chelsea stopped him.

"No, leave them on," she said, shoving him back down to the floor and covering his body with hers. "You'll be fulfilling a secret fantasy of mine—I've always wanted to make love to a man who was naked except for a pair of black dress socks."

Dakota's blue eyes danced. "You're a crazy woman, Chelsea Stone."

"And you're gonna love it, Mr. Stuffed-Shirt Law," she promised.

Taking control, she moved to accommodate the hard insistence probing against her belly. Sitting astride him, she lowered her body and slipped his penis inside her.

He jerked beneath her at the contact. "Sweetheart, you feel like heaven. So wet, so ready for me. Please . . ." he begged.

But she captured his wrists at his sides and bade him be still while she slid her lithe body back and forth along him. Her movements were exquisitely slow, sensual torture.

"I can't—" He lost control, biting down on his lip while he threw his head back and arched up with a powerful thrust. A loud groan of pleasure escaped his lips as he went rigid, suspended in the moment of mind-numbing satisfaction.

She felt him contract inside her, felt him shudder, and it tripped her own response. She came, then, with a series of little pants that exploded in spiraling points of intense gratification.

"Was I right?" she asked a few minutes later when they had caught their breath.

"I don't think anything gets any righter than we just were."

Chelsea smiled with satisfaction.

"It's too bad it was nothing more than just a game to you."

"What?" Chelsea exclaimed, moving away from him.

"I said, it was too bad it was nothing more than a game to you."

"You really believe that?" she asked, hurt and anger fueling her move to collect her items of clothing scattered on the floor.

"Shouldn't I?"

She stood before him with her clothing in the crook of her arm. "How can you . . . how can you say that?" she protested.

"I can say it because you get your jollies leading on two men. You get me so besotted, I lose my head and forget it's you and Tucker who are a team. I'm just the patsy. I've had to remind myself now that the flare of passion has cooled that you're using me for your career, that you want a song—not me."

"That's rich, Dakota. You make these terrible accusations because you can't or won't admit your feelings for me. You're too busy protecting a heart you don't have. You . . . you . . . can just go to hell, Dakota." She turned and stormed out of the kitchen. A moment later he heard her slam the door to her bedroom. The sound reverberated endlessly in his mind.

CHELSEA AWOKE TO THE sound of scratching on her bedroom door.

She rubbed her eyes and peered at the clock on the night table.

It was almost noon!

She sprang out of bed. She'd planned to be up and gone early. Though she'd considered it, leaving in the middle of the night was a bit dramatic even for her. And she'd wanted to track down Tucker to let him know they were checking out of Dakota's digs.

The scratching persisted, and she went to the door. She half expected to see Pokey's master standing beside her, an apology on his lips for believing she would lead two men on.

It had been wishful thinking on her part. The dog was alone and looking for someone to play with. She had her tennis ball in her mouth and a hopeful look in her eyes.

"Come on in, Pokey. You can help me pack."

"Pack? What's going on?" a raspy male voice demanded.

Chelsea turned to see Tucker come hobbling into the room on crutches.

"We're leaving," Chelsea said shortly. She pulled on a pair of jeans and tucked in the T-shirt she'd slept in.

Tucker eased himself down into a nearby chair, then leaned his crutches against the wall. Pokey bounded over to him, her tail wagging, the tennis ball in her mouth. Tucker took the ball and tossed it for her to catch.

"Are we leaving of our own accord, or were we invited to leave?" Tucker asked, as Pokey dropped the ball in his lap and waited for him to toss it again.

Chelsea went to the closet and began pulling her things off hangers. "Dakota Law is an egotistical, puritanical snob," she announced. She fired clothes into her open suitcase as she spoke.

"Yeah, but why are we moving out?" Tucker asked as he continued his game of catch with Pokey. "You knew Dakota's finer points before you moved in."

Chelsea stopped what she was doing and turned to Tucker.

"You want to know why we're moving out?"

"Bingo." He grinned to infuriate her even more.

"We're moving out because I've decided Dakota's never going to write a song for me."

"So, Dakota told you no and made it stick—is that what happened?" he asked.

Chelsea wadded the underwear she'd pulled from a drawer and threw it in a ball into her suitcase. "I didn't say that. What makes you think that?" she snapped.

"That's easy. You only get this angry when someone says no to you. I don't think I know anyone else in the world who hates not getting her way as much as you do, Chelsea."

"I'm not angry," she insisted.

"Ri-ight. You're a real puddle of sweet molasses like Miss Tennessee Prom Queen, downstairs."

"Who?"

"Dakota's personal assistant."

"She's here?"

"Yeah, she had a stack of folders and they locked themselves in the library. So, if you want to sneak out, now would be a good time."

"I'm not sneaking out," she lied.

"I see. Then Dakota knows you're going?"

How could he not know she was going? He'd been a real bastard last night. "Not exactly, but he told me what he thought of me in no uncertain terms."

"You want me to beat him up?"

Chelsea stared at him and started laughing. "Yeah, with your crutches." That was the thing about Tucker, he could always make her laugh.

"So, how's the Flood-Aid concert coming?" she asked. Her packing finished, she checked the room for any forgotten items.

"Great. We've lined up sponsors and a network commitment. Performers are coming out of the woodwork to volunteer their time. Both country and rock will be well represented, thanks to Dakota."

Chelsea grumbled something disparaging under her breath, and felt small for doing it. "So what's left to be done?" She closed her suitcase and had to sit on it to lock it.

"We need to scope out a place to stage the concert." Tucker maneuvered to a standing position and retrieved his crutches.

"I'll help out with that. Heaven knows, I'm not going to be busy recording a new song. How's your leg feeling? You haven't been on it too much, have you?"

"It's a royal pain—slows me down. But it could have been a hell of a lot worse. I'm not complaining, not that you'd listen to me if I did."

"Come on, we're going where they have room service. You'll feel much better. You can order up a greasy burger and fries."

"Oh, talk dirty to me some more. . . ."

"Chocolate shake, butter-drenched popcorn, double-cheese pizza . . ." Chelsea continued, laughing as they started down the sweeping staircase to the entry hall.

When they had descended only a few steps, the door to the library opened.

Dakota's voice floated up to them, followed by Melinda's tinkling laugh.

Pokey, hearing Dakota's voice, dived through Chelsea's legs, upending her. The suitcase in her hand went sailing. As it somersaulted through the air it came unlocked and its contents rained everywhere.

Pokey, delighted with this new game, chased a balled pair of socks that rolled toward Dakota's feet.

Dakota bent to retrieve the socks from Pokey's mouth, then looked to where Chelsea was scrambling to her feet on the stairs.

"What . . . what's going on?" he asked.

"We were decorating for our going-away party," Tucker said. "Looks kinda festive, don't you think?"

Dakota glanced around. His eyes came to rest on the chandelier, where an item from Chelsea's suitcase had landed. "Oh, my," Melinda said from beside him.

Chelsea's gaze followed his and her stomach sank.

· Her red teddy was draped over one of the chandelier candles.

Ignoring it, she scrambled to pick up the scattered contents of her suitcase.

Dakota bent to help her while Tucker made his way down the stairs. They gathered everything in quick order while Melinda looked on with distaste.

"We'll need a ladder," Dakota said, glancing up at what Chelsea was trying valiantly to pretend wasn't snagged on the chandelier.

"I could try to use my crutch to bat it down," Tucker offered.

"Never mind," Chelsea said, steering him toward the door. "You can keep it as a souvenir, Dakota."

"A souvenir?" Tucker echoed, sliding her a look as they went outside.

"Just keep walking, Cheesebrain."

CHELSEA SAT ALONE IN her room at the Opryland Hotel. Tucker had gone out to meet with someone about the concert. She'd begged off because she was still too wrung out by what had happened between her and Dakota.

The day was gray and rainy. It suited her mood. Her future looked equally bleak.

There wasn't going to be any song from Dakota.

She'd thought she'd had her future all figured out. Thought she'd known what she was doing.

Tucker hadn't been any help. He kept telling her that she didn't need Dakota.

She lay down across the bed and read the card.

Roses are red,
Violets are blue.
Don't let Dakota
Get to you.

It was much too late to take the good advice.
He'd gotten to her.

DAKOTA SAT IN THE dressing room of his club, Dakota Country. He'd thought maybe singing would put him in a happier frame of mind. It hadn't. He'd just been going through the motions onstage.

For the first time in his life he was lonely. Hell, he'd been lonely with a crowd of people applauding him tonight.

It was time for him to ask himself some hard questions.

Chelsea had accused him of being unable to be close to people. That he distanced himself as a form of protection.

What the hell had she meant by that? he wondered, all the while knowing the answer in his gut.

Chelsea had seen through to his fear of being hurt. Had seen past the facade that hid the pain of his family's rejection.

Perhaps because she'd also been hurt, she recognized the reasons for the barriers he put up to avoid true intimacy. She'd gotten him to talk about his family—something he never did. They hadn't just made small talk; they'd connected.

And when they'd made love . . . Well, that had certainly blown him away. She'd been open and vulnerable with him. All he could ever have hoped for.

What made him crazy was the fact that he couldn't possess her; that she shared those same things with Tucker.

The problem with him was that he believed in true love.

And worse, it didn't stop him from loving Chelsea with all his heart, even though his head told him he was crazy.

So much for all her advice about how he had to feel with his heart, instead of thinking with his head. All he'd gotten for his trouble was heart-ache.

There was a knock at the door and he snarled, "Come in."

Burt ambled into the dressing room, looking cautious.

"Yes, what is it?" Dakota asked, aware that he'd been meaner than a pit bull to everyone around him because he was eaten up with jealousy over Tucker Gable.

His loneliness intensified with every passing hour now that Chelsea had opted out of his life. She was a real pain in the butt, yet perversely he sorely missed her bugging him at every turn.

"A fan wanted you to autograph a T-shirt for her," the drummer told him, tossing Dakota the shirt. "She's a real pretty redhead," he added.

Dakota sighed. He was happy to autograph the T-shirt; it was just that it underlined how lonely being famous could be: Everybody loved you, and no one did.

After Burt left with the shirt, he shrugged out of his jacket, getting ready to go home. Home, Dakota thought gloomily, where only Pokey waited for him.

He decided he needed another drink.

Melinda Jackson entered as he was pouring a glass of Scotch.

"Don't you think you've had enough?"

"Are you talking to me?" Dakota asked. He downed the contents of the glass, then looked at her belligerently, clearly spoiling for a fight.

She walked toward him in a cloud of flowery perfume, but her eyes were bright and angry.

"Why are you sitting here feeling sorry for yourself?" she said acidly. If he wanted a fight she was ready, had been ready ever since finding Chelsea Stone ensconced in Dakota's home—the home she'd decided would be hers.

Her cotton-candy-pink nails began undoing the buttons of his shirt.

"I can get my own buttons. You don't need to take care of me, I'm perfectly sober," he insisted, pushing her hands away.

"But you do need me, Dakota." She splayed her hands on his golden-furred chest when he tossed his shirt aside.

"You're being stupid mooning like a schoolboy over trash like Chelsea Stone. Can't you see that she's making a fool of you?"

Melinda dared to press her lips to Dakota's, taking advantage of his lack of sobriety.

"Come on, Dakota, you know I'm right for you. I'll do anything for you," she promised, boldly unzipping his pants.

She kissed him again, then began licking his ear as she whispered her trump card.

"Don't let Chelsea make a fool of you, Dakota. She's probably with Tucker Gable right now."

Maybe Melinda was right, Dakota thought.

Maybe he should let Melinda seduce him as she seemed hell-bent on doing.

Maybe he'd be better off if he went back to thinking and feeling with his groin.

To hell with his heart. Damn thing was broken anyway, and likely to stay that way.

But then a picture of Chelsea and Tucker *together* flashed into his mind and jealousy propelled him out of his languid acceptance of Melinda's seduction.

He set Melinda aside, and reached for his Stetson and the bottle of Scotch.

"Where are you going?" she sputtered. "You're going to her, aren't you?"

He didn't answer.

"Why are you going to her? I'm the one who's good for you. She doesn't love you."

"But I love her. I'm foolishly and hopelessly in love with Chelsea Stone. There. I've said it."

"Damn you."

"You're probably right. I am damned." He handed her the bottle of Scotch, turned and left.

He strolled down Music Row searching for an open restaurant. He needed coffee to clear his head. He came to one that was open twenty-four hours a day, shoved his Stetson low on his head and remembered in the nick of time to zip his fly before going inside.

He was in luck. The restaurant wasn't busy. It was easy for him to stake out a table far enough away from any of the other customers that he wouldn't be noticed.

The waitress who came up to him was young, efficient and recognized him. She quickly sensed that he wanted to remain anonymous.

He nodded his appreciation when she returned with a decanter of hot coffee.

He read her name tag, Lilybet, before she left to take a check to a pair of lovebirds who were in dire need of a motel room, if they didn't want to be arrested for indecent exposure.

He drank a cup of black coffee and watched Lilybet dispatch the couple without having to toss a pitcher of cold water on them.

Lilybet was a blond amazon, quite the opposite of the willowy brunette haunting his mind—Chelsea Stone, the woman with a heart of stone . . . He reached for a napkin and signaled the waitress.

He pulled a twenty-dollar bill from his wallet. "I'll give you this for your pencil," he offered, sliding the money across the table.

"Sure," she agreed. She pulled the pencil from behind her ear, handed it over, and picked up the money. "Let me know if you need anything else."

He didn't hear her. His head was bent in concentration as he scribbled madly on the napkin, afraid he wouldn't be able to jot down the fragments of lyric spinning around in his head before he lost them.

When he was done, he didn't have a song, but he was closer to one than he had been in a long while.

He slid another twenty from his wallet and motioned the waitress to come back.

"You a singer, Lilybet?"

She nodded.

"How long have you been in Nashville?"

"Two years," she answered, a little apologetic that she'd never considered leaving when she hadn't found early success.

He could have told her it was the artists who never gave up that were the ones who succeeded— some sooner than others, but most, eventually.

Quitting was the easy way out.

Dakota pulled a business card from his wallet and used her pencil to write a personal message on the back of the card. He laid the card down on top of the twenty.

"Keep the change, Lilybet, and call the man whose name I wrote down for you on the back of the card. He scouts talent for my record company. Tell him I said to give you an audition."

"Mr. Law!" Lilybet's hand went to her mouth to cover her happy surprise. "I don't know how to thank you."

"Don't be thanking me yet. My record company's not that thrilled with me right now because my new album's a little late. But that won't stop them from giving you a listen. Especially when you pass on a message from me."

"A message?"

"Just tell him I think I have the final song for the album," he said, picking up the napkin he'd scribbled on and tucking it in his pocket.

"I'll do that. And I was wondering, would you autograph the back of this tab for me?"

He did just that, and wished her good luck as he left.

His head was clear, but he hadn't changed his mind about going to the Opryland Hotel to see Chelsea. He was going to tell her that he loved her.

Not because he wanted to.

Not because he thought it was a particularly good idea.

And not because he wanted to prove anything to her.

But because he couldn't *not* tell her.

When he arrived at the Opryland Hotel he'd practiced twenty-three ways to tell her. All of them escaped him as he walked across the patterned green carpet in the foyer, past the marble-topped tables and plush furniture.

His eyes were fastened on the big winding staircase and giant chandelier in the hotel lobby. They reminded him of Chelsea's exit from his home. It had certainly been dramatic. Despite his mood, the corner of his mouth twitched. He didn't think he'd ever be able to look at a chandelier again and not see a red lace teddy hanging from it in his mind's eye.

He took a deep breath and headed for the registration desk. He had to find Chelsea now before he lost his nerve; before he could make rationalizations for why he should avoid the possibility of rejection.

He knew that this time, he was putting all his chips on the table. If he lost, he wasn't sure it was a loss he'd ever recover from.

"Are you sure?" he asked when the desk clerk told him Chelsea had gone.

"Yes, sir. She and the gentleman checked out this evening."

"Where did they go? Did she say where they were going?"

"I don't know. They took the hotel shuttle to the airport, I believe."

Dakota turned away from the desk.

He hadn't expected it; had been completely unprepared to find her gone. He walked past the hotel shops to the conservatory, then wandered the paths aimlessly, looking up at the wrought-iron balconies and bay windows of the luxury suites.

He imagined Chelsea standing on one of the balconies. He would have climbed that balcony, been ready to play Romeo to her Juliet. He had been prepared to risk everything for true love, but there was no true love to woo.

She'd made her choice and left with Tucker.

There was nothing for him to do but go home. The ride back was the longest one of his life. It didn't help that it was filled with memories of the times Chelsea had made the drive with him.

When he arrived home at last, he was as blue as he'd ever been. Loneliness had a new name—Chelsea Stone. And it didn't escape him that the word that rhymed best with *Stone* was . . . *alone*.

He called Pokey but she didn't come. He found her curled up on the bed in the room Chelsea had used.

The dog looked up at him with sad brown eyes.

Dakota flopped down on the bed beside her. "Yeah, I miss her, too," he said.

11

"Looks like you've got a sell-out crowd here for the Flood-Aid concert," the interviewer from The Nashville Network said, as he wrapped up the pre-concert interview with Chelsea and Tucker. TNN had been heavily promoting the benefit on the Crook and Chase show, "American Music Shop" and "Nashville Now."

Tucker shook the interviewer's hand. "Appreciate your support, man. Hope you enjoy the concert. We rounded up a lotta country artists, but there's gonna be a little bit of rock and roll, too."

"Does that mean Chelsea Stone is going to join you onstage?" the interviewer asked, looking to her for a reply.

"She has to help hold me up, don't you, babe?" Tucker hobbled over to her on his walking cast and laid his arm across her shoulders.

Chelsea's smile was forced.

"What will you be singing? Rumor has it you're crossing over to country, Chelsea. Are you planning to debut some country material tonight?"

"I think the crowd wants to hear my hits," Chelsea said, evading the question.

"I know I do," the interviewer agreed, letting her off the hook.

"Well, it's time to get the show on the road," Tucker said, giving the interviewer his cue that it was time to cut the tape.

"Ready?" Tucker asked, turning to Chelsea.

"Why don't you go on first with your band. I need to powder my nose, touch up my lipstick, and maybe toss my cookies," she said with a weak grin.

"Are you all right?" Tucker looked at her closely.

"I'm fine. I'm fine," she assured him. "Go melt some hearts."

"Promise you'll prop me up, if I fall over?" he coaxed, bussing her nose with a kiss. "I feel like a turtle on its back when I try to get up with this damn cast on."

"It's good for you. It'll teach you patience."

Tucker laughed. "Yeah. I'm likely to learn patience like you're likely to learn patience. We're the poster couple for instant gratification."

The packed Busch Memorial Stadium sounded like the St. Louis Cardinals were playing a World Series game when Clint Black strolled onstage and motioned for Tucker to join him.

Clint tested the microphones and then Tucker stood beside him and the screaming intensified. When they got the crowd settled down, Tucker took over the mike.

"Before we start the concert, I want to thank everyone in the music business who contributed to this effort to help the flood victims recover from the disaster. We picked St. Louis because it's where the Missouri River and the Mississippi merge, and flooded their banks, wreaking havoc on this community. Tonight, ladies and gentlemen, rock and country are gonna merge, and while we might wreak a little havoc, we're gonna do a lot of good.

"The music will start in a few minutes. But first Clint and I are going to show you the things that were contributed by the celebrities here tonight for a silent auction. The place to send your bids will be flashed on the electronic scoreboard."

The music stars had contributed everything from an autographed saddle to an electric guitar. When the items for auction ran out, Tucker said, "Now I'm gonna let Clint here ease us into the night with his first hit single, 'Better Man.'" He left the stage and Clint's soulful voice sliced into the clear St. Louis night.

Tucker stood on the sidelines talking to Clint's actress wife, Lisa Hartman, trying to coax her into singing with her husband later. Clint gave Tucker the evil eye, then smiled.

Clint moved on to do another of his hits, "Put Yourself in My Shoes," and then Bruce Springsteen took the stage with his hard-rocking band, which set the format of alternating country and rock.

Reba McEntire managed a spangled costume change between her two songs, Lyle Lovett brought along his Pretty Woman and sang to her while every nonhunk in the audience cheered, and the new band Bella Donna, wearing enough silver jewelry to plate a Buick, looked like a walking advertisement for Chrome Heart.

It was finally time for Tucker and Chelsea.

They took the stage and turned up the heat.

When they finished their first number, Tucker leaned into the mike, stretched out his leg with the cast and yelled to the crowd of fifty thousand that it was time to "kick some ass."

The crowd cheered as he and Chelsea did a medley of Motown hits with a rendition of Marvin Gaye's "Sexual Healing" that was hotter than a firecracker on the Fourth of July.

Chelsea moved like a cat in her skintight black catsuit and bangled neon-blue bolero top.

The audience cheered and stamped their feet until it felt like the New Madrid fault had triggered a trembler.

It was a hard act to follow.

Clint Black took the stage, then, to announce the last performance of the evening.

"Ladies and gentlemen, we have a surprise performer—Dakota Law."

Chelsea stood on the sidelines with Tucker watching as Dakota took the stage and waited for the wild applause to die down.

"Why didn't you tell me he was going to be here?" she demanded.

"If I had, it wouldn't have been a surprise, now would it?"

"You should have told me."

Tucker wrapped his arm around her and pulled her to his side. "Oh now, don't pout, babe. You can't be having your way all the time. People would say I was a wuss, and we can't have that. I've got my bad reputation to uphold, just like you."

Chelsea socked his arm.

"Quit that," he grumbled as Dakota cleared his throat and began speaking into the mike.

"I think we should all give Tucker Gable a round of applause for getting this benefit together. As you know, the proceeds from tonight will go to aid the flood victims."

Tucker waved away the spotlight when it searched him out, and waved to acknowledge the crowd's cheers.

"And now," Dakota said, taking the mike off the stand, "now I'd like to perform the new single from my album, which will be released next month. It's called 'Heart of Stone.'"

"I thought you said he was still blocked," Tucker whispered.

Chelsea didn't say a word, just stood with her gaze fixed on Dakota as he began a torch song that packed a powerhouse wallop. It was unabashedly romantic.

Chelsea was not amused.

It didn't take half a brain to figure out "Heart of Stone" was about Chelsea Stone. She could feel everyone's gaze shift from Dakota to her.

"Well, I'll be damned," Tucker declared beside her.

"Shut up, Cheesebrain."

Dakota held the crowd in the palm of his hand as he finished up the nakedly emotional song.

"Is that a tear? I think that's a tear," Tucker said as Dakota sang the closing verse.

"Tucker, shut up," Chelsea said through clenched teeth.

The audience was silent when Dakota finished his song. Clearly, the achingly personal lyrics of heartbreak had touched everyone.

And then the audience's applause swelled to a crescendo as Dakota left the stage—applause that continued as the crowd demanded an encore.

Wynonna picked up on the fact that Dakota was in no shape to go back out onstage alone. She grabbed his hand and nodded to Clint and his wife to join them. The other performers followed suit until the stage was filled with everyone singing "God Bless America."

After the applause died down, the performers milled about onstage, talking and hugging, while the crowd began to file out of the stadium.

Dakota disentangled himself and headed in Chelsea's direction.

When she saw him, she quickly averted her glance. "Come on, Tucker, let's blow this Popsicle stand," she said, tugging his arm.

Dakota called out her name.

She pretended not to hear. Everyone turned to look—not at him but at Chelsea. Undaunted, he headed after her.

He called her name again, louder this time. More insistently.

Now people weren't just looking, they were staring.

"Chelsea, answer the man," Tucker coaxed. "Behave yourself, for once."

She turned reluctantly to acknowledge Dakota before he called any more attention to them.

"Helluva song, man," Tucker said, slapping Dakota on the back when he reached them. "I've got to wind things up with Clint. Catch you later."

Chelsea and Dakota stood alone, looking at each other.

Finally she broke the silence between them. "The answer is no."

"I haven't said what I wanted," Dakota said, his voice husky.

"I'll tell you what, I'll agree to talk to you on one condition—you agree that after I listen to what you have to say and then tell you no, you'll go."

"How do you know you'll say no?" he drawled.

"Easy. Only a fool would say yes to a man like you. And I'm no longer a fool, Dakota Law."

He tipped his white Stetson with his forefinger and looked at her, his blue eyes fathomless.

"Are we agreed?" she prompted.

He grumbled his reply.

"I take it eat dirt and die is a no?"

He turned to disappear into the crowd.

"Not so fast, cowboy."

He stopped in his tracks and looked back over his shoulder at her, waiting.

"You still owe me a song."

"Do I?"

"You're over your writer's block."

"Am I?"

"That song was about me. You didn't know me six months ago. It's a new song."

"I just finished it last night."

"I thought you said it was going to be on your new album."

"It is, I just haven't recorded it yet."

"Good. You can give it to me."

"On one condition..." He turned to face her. "We sing the song together on my album."

"A duet?"

He nodded.

"I NEVER THOUGHT you'd agree to do this, Chelsea," Dakota said, as the private plane he'd chartered lifted off the runway on the return flight from St. Louis to Nashville.

"And I never thought you'd mention my name again, much less sing it in front of fifty thousand people," Chelsea said. "You really put yourself on the line tonight. Why did you do it?"

"Why did you agree to come with me tonight and record the duet with me? Was it just a career move, or something more?" he asked, taking her hand.

He felt her hand grip his as they hit an air pocket and the plane dropped for a second or two before adjusting itself.

She smiled weakly. "I guess you might as well know about one of my shameful secrets. Much as I hate to admit it, I'm a white-knuckle flyer."

He grinned at her. "Now that's a surprise. The wrestler's grip you have on my hand didn't give you away at all. Does this mean if we run into a little turbulence, I can expect to find you in my lap?" he asked hopefully.

She ignored his questions as the plane settled into a smooth ride in the starlit darkness. She relaxed her grip, but he continued to hold her hand possessively.

"You didn't answer my question," he said, returning to their earlier conversation.

"You won't find me in your lap," she said, evasive and exasperating as hell.

He was in too much pain to keep up their usual guarded banter. "That's not what I meant, and you know it. Did you come with me tonight because it would be a good career move, Chelsea?"

"I came because I always do what's good for me," Chelsea replied, not willing to give away any more than he was. "I've had to take care of myself from a very early age. I think your idea of doing the song as a duet is a great marketing angle that will work for both of us."

"So you came because of your career. You came because what you want from me is what you said you wanted all along—a song."

She didn't answer him.

He was quiet for a few minutes, then reached for his briefcase. He opened it and withdrew some sheet music. "In that case, maybe we should practice it now so we'll be ready in the morning when we go into the studio to record it. The musicians have already laid down the track. I've booked two three-hour sessions, just in case we need a backup. But with any luck we can get it done in one and you can be home with Tucker by tomorrow night."

"Tucker's going back out on tour tomorrow. He might even get his cast off. Except, knowing him, he'll ask for a new one because he's enjoying all the attention it gets him."

"Well, you'll need to be home anyway, in that case," Dakota said glumly.

"What do you mean?"

"You know, to be there to sign for all the cards, flowers and lingerie Tucker showers you with. Guess any man would find Tucker Gable a hard act to follow. No wonder he has your heart sewn up."

"Is that what you think? You think Tucker and I are lovers because of our stage act? Do you think mystery writers go out and kill people because they write about it? Do you think every actor and actress who do a love scene together also do it for real? Come on, Dakota, you can't possibly be that unsophisticated."

"You've never denied it. The press has rumored the two of you were lovers from the start. I only know what I see when the two of you are onstage burning it up together."

"And what do you see?" she asked, very quietly.

"I see red. I see you with Tucker and I want it to be me. I'm jealous. I'm out of my mind with jealousy over Tucker Gable. There, I've said it." He looked away from her and stared out the plane window, his mood as dark as the night.

"It could be you, Dakota," she whispered.

"What?" He turned to look at her, half afraid he was hearing things.

"I said, it could be you. Tucker and I are not lovers, Dakota. I love Tucker, but I'm not in love with him."

"But...but does he know? He signs all the things he sends you, 'Love, Me.' I thought—"

"You should have asked me instead of just assuming the worst. Assuming I was the kind of woman who would lead on two men. That hurts, Dakota. Tucker and I are like family. We practically raised each other. We care deeply about each other, and we both appreciate each other's sexuality. But we aren't lovers. Neither of us is willing to risk losing the only family either of us has."

"And that's why he sends you all the presents he does—because he's the only family you have?"

Chelsea shook her head. "Those presents aren't from Tucker." She laughed. "Except for the truly trashy salt-and-pepper shakers he sends when he's on the road."

"You mean there's someone else?"

"They're from me, Dakota," she confessed, putting him out of his misery.

"What?"

"They're from me. It's like I told you—I've had to take care of myself from an early age. So I developed the habit of nurturing myself. I send myself cards...."

"What kind of cards?"

"They can be any kind that makes me feel better." She chuckled. "I remember this one card. It was one of those really sweet, flowery, in-touch-with-your-feelings type of card. It said, 'I don't know what you're going through, but I care.'"

"You're a crazy woman, Chelsea Stone," Dakota said, laughing.

"Actually, I think it's an incredibly sane thing to do. We all need to take better care of ourselves. Maybe we'd start treating others better, too, if we did."

"So you love flowers, and lingerie. What else do you love?"

"Bears. I especially love teddy bears."

"That's it?"

"All I can think of," she answered, still unwilling to admit her feelings for him when she wasn't certain his went past jealousy.

Screwing up his courage, Dakota blurted out the words he'd never said to anyone: "I love you."

Her lip trembled. "I thought you were never going to say it," she said, her eyes glassy as he pulled her into his arms.

"I love you, too, Dakota Law," she whispered, as he crushed her against him in a breathless hug, mumbling something against her ear.

"What are you saying?"

"Hush, I'm praying for turbulence."

"You don't need to do that."

"Really?"

She smiled and shook her head. A wicked look gleamed in her dark eyes.

"Fetch me that blanket and pillow from the seat over there," she told him.

"Are you saying what I think you're saying?" he asked, reaching for the blanket.

"Just get the blanket."

"But . . ."

"Oh, for heaven's sake, Dakota. There aren't any other passengers. No one is going to see us. Haven't you ever done anything like this before?"

"No."

"Well, I guess I'm going to be a bad influence on you, then."

Dakota groaned. If Chelsea was confident before, now, knowing he loved her, she was cocky as hell. He was going to be in for some turbulent times—and he was looking forward to them with great joy.

"But what if the pilot comes back to use the bathroom or something and catches us?" he argued, but spread the blanket over them nevertheless.

"Then we'll just have to kill him so he doesn't sell the story to the tabloids," she said matter-of-factly, nibbling on his ear.

"Aren't you forgetting something?" he asked, groaning as she pressed her hand against his straining fly.

"You mean protection?"

"No. I mean, if we kill the pilot, who's going to fly the plane?"

"Okay, so we let him live. We just make him promise not to tell your mother."

"Deal," Dakota agreed, chuckling until she made a bold forage at his zipper.

"Dakota?"

"Uh-hmm . . . ?"

"Do you think your mother is going to like me?"

"*What!*"

"I asked if you thought your mother was going to like me. You are planning to take me home to meet your family, aren't you?"

The look on his face went from shock to amusement and was followed by a deep, satisfying belly laugh. "You know what? I am."

"Dakota?"

"What?"

"This isn't going to work for me." She shifted in her seat.

"Why not? 'Cause I got to tell you, it really works for me."

"Because this outfit is all one piece. I'm going to have to stand on my head to get out of it."

"Lost your nerve, have you?"

"Are you daring me, Dakota?"

"I'm daring you."

With that she threw off the blanket and stepped into the aisle where she had enough room to peel out of the tight black cat-suit.

"You have any other dares you want to try out on me?" she demanded, standing before him with her hands on her naked hips.

"I might have just one or two—but I think I'll save them."

"Why?"

"Because the Fasten Seat Belts sign just lit up," he said, nodding toward the front of the cabin. He caught her as the plane gave a lurch and she fell into his lap.

"My prayers were answered," he said, wrapping her in an encompassing embrace and pulling the blanket back over them.

"Dakota, I can't do this now!"

"Sure, you can. It will take your mind off the turbulence."

His hands began roaming over her body beneath the soft blue blanket, driving her to distraction. She squirmed and gave tiny squeals of delight—noises he muffled with his deep, slaking kisses.

"You're going to have to learn to control those squeals that give us away, sweetheart, if you want to continue making love in public places.

And then he moaned as she shoved his pants down to his ankles and stroked him. "Hush," she countered. "You have to learn to control yourself."

His answer was to pull her astride him. The scent of his spicy cologne, her sweet perfume and sex mingled to permeate the air surrounding them, suffusing it with an erotic, electric charge that enhanced the very public private act they were lost in.

She wrapped herself around his hardness and slid back and forth in his lap, wet and easy.

"I love it like this, Chelsea," he whispered hoarsely. "Every time I go into the kitchen I remember us together on the floor."

Chelsea giggled and licked his throat. "I suppose one of these days we really ought to try a bed for novelty."

She moaned then as he squeezed her buttocks and thrust into her deeply. She trembled around him and cried out, gripping his powerful shoulders with her hands.

He teased her, thrusting slowly, withholding what she wanted until she begged prettily.

And then the minx, when she'd climaxed and he was climbing the crest of passion, said, "Did you hear that? Is that the pilot?"

His eyes flew open as he arched into a shattering climax of his own.

He looked into her eyes and saw that she was very satisfied with herself.

This was a woman who was going to keep him on his toes, drive him nuts and make him happy. This was true love.

THE PILOT DIDN'T comment when Dakota carried a sleeping Chelsea off the plane, wrapped in a blanket.

He was taking care of her.

Something that made him feel very good. He'd needed that in his life.

Someone to take care of, someone to take care of him.

Someone to care.

When the limo pulled up to his house, he carried her inside and upstairs.

Pokey jumped down from the bed, wagging her tail and yipping.

"Yes, girl. I've brought her home.

"Home to stay."

12

CHELSEA AWOKE TO THE sun streaming into the bedroom.

Dakota's bedroom.

As she rubbed her eyes, Pokey jumped up on the bed and lay at her feet with her tail thumping. The dog looked as if she were grinning. Looked like she was happy to see her.

She reached down to pet the dog, who took it as a cue to go find her tennis ball for a game of catch.

The pillow beside her had not been slept on. Had Dakota had second thoughts? Where was he?

She didn't have to wait long for the answer.

Within minutes, Pokey came bounding back with her yellow tennis ball in her mouth. She jumped back up on the bed and dropped it in Chelsea's lap.

"Okay, okay, I'm getting up. We'll go outside and play, you silly animal."

Pokey yipped for her to hurry.

She threw back the blankets.

"Oopsies. I can't go outside. I don't seem to have any clothes on."

"A capital way to start the morning, if you ask me." Dakota strolled into the bedroom with a towel wrapped low on his lean hips and carrying a white wicker bed tray from which the most scrumptious aroma wafted.

"I had the cook make us cinnamon French toast, fresh-squeezed orange juice, hot Swiss coffee and strawberries and cream."

"I take it you have a treadmill. . . ."

"Actually, I have a more enjoyable method in mind for burning off the calories," he said with a wicked wink. He set the tray down in front of her and whisked off his towel.

He leaned over the bed, picked up the yellow tennis ball and threw it into the hall where it bounced down the winding staircase. "Go fetch, Pokey."

They both laughed as Pokey tried to make up her mind between the smells coming from the tray and her beloved tennis ball. The tennis ball won out and dishes clattered as she leaped off the bed and bounded from the room in search of it.

They sat in bed feeding each other between passionate kisses. The syrup wandered from the plate to their bodies and had to be licked off amid slaps and giggles.

The doorbell peeled and Pokey set up a commotion in the foyer.

"I'd better go see who that is before Pokey lets them in so she'll have someone to play with," Dakota said. He rolled out of bed and pulled on a white terry-cloth robe. "Keep my place and remember where we left off, will you?" He bent to brush a kiss on her nose, then headed downstairs.

Chelsea waited, enjoying a spoonful of strawberries and cream. And then she laid down the spoon with a clatter. What if it was Melinda Jackson? She didn't want to be found naked in Dakota's bed by his assistant.

She got out of bed, went to Dakota's huge walk-in closet, selected one of his white shirts and slipped it on.

"I thought I told you to keep my place," Dakota said, coming up behind her as she folded the sleeves back over her wrists.

"Who was it?" she asked, buttoning the shirt.

"A deliveryman."

"Oh."

"It was for you."

She turned. "For me?"

He nodded, and led her back out into the sunny bedroom where a giant teddy bear sat on a chair. Pokey stood beside it, looking up at it quizzically.

Chelsea started to cry.

"Now, now. Teddy bears aren't supposed to make you cry. You'll hurt his feelings."

Sniffling, she went across the room to the stuffed animal that Pokey was now sniffing suspiciously.

There was a card in the bear's paws.

Chelsea looked back over her shoulder to Dakota.

"Open it."

She picked up the envelope, slipped the card from the envelope and read.

Marry me.
I dare you.

Love, Me

She started to cry again.

"Oh, hell, I guess that means the answer is no, Pokey."

Chelsea shook her head, ran across the room and threw herself into his arms.

"The answer is yes. Yes, yes, yes, yes."

Pokey barked as Dakota swung Chelsea around.

"We're getting married, girl. Go fetch. Go fetch my jacket."

The dog dragged Dakota's jacket from the chair and brought it to him.

Dakota took a small black velvet box from his jacket pocket. After flipping open the lid, he held it out for Chelsea to see.

"Dakota! It's so beautiful," she cried, tears welling in her eyes again. "But it's early morning. You couldn't have been to a jeweler's."

Dakota smiled, pleased she liked the square-cut diamond flanked by two rubies that sparkled in the bright morning sunlight.

"I've had the ring for weeks. I just didn't have the nerve to come to you, to ask you to marry me until last night. Put it on your finger for me."

Chelsea slipped the sparkling gem on the third finger of her left hand. "I'm engaged to be married. I can't believe it." Grinning from ear to ear, she threw her arms around his neck and kissed him.

"I have to call Tucker and tell him," she said, stepping back.

After getting the number where Tucker could be reached from his service, she dialed and got through.

"Hello, Tucker. Guess what. I'm getting married!"

"I know, babe. Congratulations."

"What do you mean, you know?" she demanded, looking at Dakota.

"Your groom-to-be called me and asked my permission for your hand in marriage this morning. He said you'd told him I was your only family. You got yourself a proper suitor there, babe."

"What did you tell him, Tucker?" she coaxed.

"I gave him my permission, of course. But I gave it on one condition."

"What condition?" she demanded, her eyes narrowing as she waited for his reply.

"That I get to be best man at your wedding, of course. You know I seldom wear a tuxedo, but I do look rather dashing in one, if I do say so myself."

"But of course, you'll be the best man," she agreed. And then her dark eyes sparkled. "And, if you get with the program, maybe we can even make it a double wedding. Marriage is 'in' in the nineties, Tucker."

"Goodbye, babe. I'll talk to you later when the champagne wears off."

Chelsea hung up the phone. "Tucker thought we were drinking champagne. Imagine, at this hour!"

"We'll have champagne at the studio after we record our duet this afternoon," Dakota promised.

Chelsea wrung her hands. "I'm nervous as a cat in a room full of rocking chairs."

Dakota laughed. "About the duet, or about marrying me?"

"Both."

"I'm not letting you change your mind about either," he vowed. "In fact, if I have my way there'll be a lot of songs we sing together."

"What are you talking about?"

"My record company is considering trying an album like the classic with Tammy Wynette and George Jones."

"Are you asking what I think you're asking?"

"I want you to be my partner in every area of my life, Chelsea."

"Aren't you worried that we'll be spending too much time together?"

"Sweetheart, I've spent enough time alone."

HARLEQUIN®

Temptation

Lost Loves

RIGHT MAN...WRONG TIME

Remember that one man who turned your world upside down? Who made you experience all the ecstatic highs of passion and lows of loss and regret. What if you met him again?

You dared to lose your heart once and had it broken. Dare you love again?

JoAnn Ross, Glenda Sanders, Rita Clay Estrada, Gina Wilkins and Carin Rafferty. Find their stories in Lost Loves, Temptation's newest miniseries, running May to September 1994.

In June, experience *WHAT MIGHT HAVE BEEN* by Glenda Sanders. Barbara had never forgotten her high school sweetheart—nor forgiven him. Richard had gotten another girl pregnant and dutifully married her. Now a single dad, he's back in town, hoping to recapture and rekindle...what might have been.

What if...?

Available in June wherever Harlequin books are sold.

Fifty red-blooded, white-hot, true-blue hunks
from every State in the Union!

Look for MEN MADE IN AMERICA! Written by some of
our most popular authors, these stories feature fifty of
the strongest, sexiest men, each from a different state in
the union!

Two titles available every other month at your favorite
retail outlet.

In May, look for:

KISS YESTERDAY GOODBYE by Leigh Michaels (Iowa)
A TIME TO KEEP by Curtiss Ann Matlock (Kansas)

In June, look for:

ONE PALE, FAWN GLOVE by Linda Shaw (Kentucky)
BAYOU MIDNIGHT by Emilie Richards (Louisiana)

You won't be able to resist MEN MADE IN AMERICA!

HARLEQUIN®

Temptation®

IS TEN!

Join the festivities as Harlequin celebrates
Temptation's tenth anniversary in 1994!

Look for tempting treats from your favorite
Temptation authors all year long. The celebration
begins with Passion's Quest—four exciting sensual
stories featuring the most elemental passions....

The temptation continues with Lost Loves, a sizzling
miniseries about love lost...love found. And watch for
the 500th Temptation in July by bestselling author
Rita Clay Estrada, a seductive story in the vein
of the much-loved tale, THE IVORY KEY.

In May, look for details of an irresistible offer:
three classic Temptation novels by Rita Clay Estrada,
Glenda Sanders and Gina Wilkins in a collector's
hardcover edition—free with proof of purchase!

After ten tempting years, *nobody* can resist

Temptation®

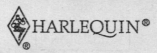

HARLEQUIN®

Don't miss these Harlequin favorites by some of our most
distinguished authors!
And now, you can receive a discount by ordering two or more titles!

HT #25551	THE OTHER WOMAN by Candace Schuler	$2.99	☐
HT #25539	FOOLS RUSH IN by Vicki Lewis Thompson	$2.99	☐
HP #11550	THE GOLDEN GREEK by Sally Wentworth	$2.89	☐
HP #11603	PAST ALL REASON by Kay Thorpe	$2.99	☐
HR #03228	MEANT FOR EACH OTHER by Rebecca Winters	$2.89	☐
HR #03268	THE BAD PENNY by Susan Fox	$2.99	☐
HS #70532	TOUCH THE DAWN by Karen Young	$3.39	☐
HS #70540	FOR THE LOVE OF IVY by Barbara Kaye	$3.39	☐
HI #22177	MINDGAME by Laura Pender	$2.79	☐
HI #22214	TO DIE FOR by M.J. Rodgers	$2.89	☐
HAR #16421	HAPPY NEW YEAR, DARLING by Margaret St. George	$3.29	☐
HAR #16507	THE UNEXPECTED GROOM by Muriel Jensen	$3.50	☐
HH #28774	SPINDRIFT by Miranda Jarrett	$3.99	☐
HH #28782	SWEET SENSATIONS by Julie Tetel	$3.99	☐

Harlequin Promotional Titles

#83259	UNTAMED MAVERICK HEARTS	$4.99	☐

(Short-story collection featuring Heather Graham Pozzessere,
Patricia Potter, Joan Johnston)
(limited quantities available on certain titles)

	AMOUNT	$
DEDUCT:	**10% DISCOUNT FOR 2+ BOOKS**	$
	POSTAGE & HANDLING	$
	($1.00 for one book, 50¢ for each additional)	
	APPLICABLE TAXES*	$ _____
	TOTAL PAYABLE	$ _____
	(check or money order—please do not send cash)	

To order, complete this form and send it, along with a check or money order for the
total above, payable to Harlequin Books, to: **In the U.S.:** 3010 Walden Avenue,
P.O. Box 9047, Buffalo, NY 14269-9047; **In Canada:** P.O. Box 613, Fort Erie, Ontario,
L2A 5X3.

Name: _____

Address: _____ City: _____

State/Prov.: _____ Zip/Postal Code: _____

*New York residents remit applicable sales taxes.
  Canadian residents remit applicable GST and provincial taxes.

HBACK-AJ

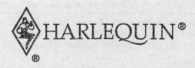

INDULGE A LITTLE 6947 SWEEPSTAKES
NO PURCHASE NECESSARY

HERE'S HOW THE SWEEPSTAKES WORKS:
The Harlequin Reader Service shipments for January, February and March 1994 will contain, respectively, coupons for entry into three prize drawings: a trip for two to San Francisco, an Alaskan cruise for two and a trip for two to Hawaii. To be eligible for any drawing using an Entry Coupon, simply complete and mail according to directions.

There is no obligation to continue as a Reader Service subscriber to enter and be eligible for any prize drawing. You may also enter any drawing by hand printing your name and address on a 3" x 5" card and the destination of the prize you wish that entry to be considered for (i.e., San Francisco trip, Alaskan cruise or Hawaiian trip). Send your 3" x 5" entries to: Indulge a Little 6947 Sweepstakes, c/o Prize Destination you wish that entry to be considered for, P.O. Box 1315, Buffalo, NY 14269-1315, U.S.A. or Indulge a Little 6947 Sweepstakes, P.O. Box 610, Fort Erie, Ontario L2A 5X3, Canada.

To be eligible for the San Francisco trip, entries must be received by 4/30/94; for the Alaskan cruise, 5/31/94; and the Hawaiian trip, 6/30/94. No responsibility is assumed for lost, late or misdirected mail. Sweepstakes open to residents of the U.S. (except Puerto Rico) and Canada, 18 years of age or older. All applicable laws and regulations apply. Sweepstakes void wherever prohibited.

For a copy of the Official Rules, send a self-addressed, stamped envelope (WA residents need not affix return postage) to: Indulge a Little 6947 Rules, P.O. Box 4631, Blair, NE 68009, U.S.A.

INDR93

INDULGE A LITTLE 6947 SWEEPSTAKES
NO PURCHASE NECESSARY

HERE'S HOW THE SWEEPSTAKES WORKS:
The Harlequin Reader Service shipments for January, February and March 1994 will contain, respectively, coupons for entry into three prize drawings: a trip for two to San Francisco, an Alaskan cruise for two and a trip for two to Hawaii. To be eligible for any drawing using an Entry Coupon, simply complete and mail according to directions.

There is no obligation to continue as a Reader Service subscriber to enter and be eligible for any prize drawing. You may also enter any drawing by hand printing your name and address on a 3" x 5" card and the destination of the prize you wish that entry to be considered for (i.e., San Francisco trip, Alaskan cruise or Hawaiian trip). Send your 3" x 5" entries to: Indulge a Little 6947 Sweepstakes, c/o Prize Destination you wish that entry to be considered for, P.O. Box 1315, Buffalo, NY 14269-1315, U.S.A. or Indulge a Little 6947 Sweepstakes, P.O. Box 610, Fort Erie, Ontario L2A 5X3, Canada.

To be eligible for the San Francisco trip, entries must be received by 4/30/94; for the Alaskan cruise, 5/31/94; and the Hawaiian trip, 6/30/94. No responsibility is assumed for lost, late or misdirected mail. Sweepstakes open to residents of the U.S. (except Puerto Rico) and Canada, 18 years of age or older. All applicable laws and regulations apply. Sweepstakes void wherever prohibited.

For a copy of the Official Rules, send a self-addressed, stamped envelope (WA residents need not affix return postage) to: Indulge a Little 6947 Rules, P.O. Box 4631, Blair, NE 68009, U.S.A.

INDR93

INDULGE A LITTLE
SWEEPSTAKES

OFFICIAL ENTRY COUPON

This entry must be received by: JUNE 30, 1994
This month's winner will be notified by: JULY 15, 1994
Trip must be taken between: AUGUST 31, 1994-AUGUST 31, 1995

YES, I want to win the 3-Island Hawaiian vacation for two. I understand that
the prize includes round-trip airfare, first-class hotels and pocket money as
revealed on the "wallet" scratch-off card.

Name_____

Address _____ Apt. _____

City_____

State/Prov._____ Zip/Postal Code_____

Daytime phone number_____
                              (Area Code)

Account #_____

Return entries with invoice in envelope provided. Each book in this shipment has two
entry coupons—and the more coupons you enter, the better your chances of winning!
© 1993 HARLEQUIN ENTERPRISES LTD.   MONTH3